FILTHY
crown

A SINGLE DAD AGE GAP ROMANCE

ELEANOR ALDRICK

FILTHY

crown

A SINGLE DAD AGE GAP ROMANCE

ELEANOR ALDRICK

Filthy Crown

Copyright © 2021 by Eleanor Aldrick

Cover Design: Sinfully Seductive Designs
Interior Formatting: Sinfully Seductive Designs
Proof Read by: Dark by Design

This is a work of fiction. Names, characters, businesses, places, events, locales, and incidents are either the products of the author's imagination or used in a fictitious manner. Any resemblance to actual persons, living or dead, or actual events is purely coincidental.

FIRST EDITION

ISBN: 9798482460788

10 9 8 7 6 5 4 3 2 1

To everyone who needs a little break from reality. May my words bring you the much needed retreat into bliss.

"Do what you want because tomorrow isn't promised and forever isn't real."

- Eleanor Aldrick

Playlist
ON REPEAT

Make it Hot - Major Lazer & Anitta

Won't Sleep - Tones And I

Upward Over the Mountain - Iron & Wine

Sorrow - The National

Bruises - Lewis Capaldi

999 - Selena Gomez & Camilo

Bells in Santa Fe - Halsey

Whispers - Halsey

Prologue

PENELOPE

"**D**on't watch." Mom's strangled sob cuts through the haze as our eyes meet through a sea of despair.

I can't do it. I can't look away.

She's bound, kneeling before us with one of our captors holding her head up–her face contorting as his meaty fingers grip tightly onto her hair.

The scene unfolding before me is one you'd expect from a horror movie, not real life. I take it all in, wondering how in the hell we got here. How did a family vacation turn into something so dark?

My stepfather's body is lying next to mom's. His head missing, nowhere to be found. Time stands still as I watch the pool of crimson, and for a second I wonder if this is all just a dream, a nightmare I can't wake from.

As if in answer, the sting of pain brings me back to the present, making me suck in a sharp breath. Looking down, I see tiny fingers digging into my arm, reminding me that this is all too real.

"Momma!" My sister's voice cracks, just like my soul.

"Please." Our mother's eyes dart between the three of us, begging us to look away. "Pen, take care of my babies."

A lump lodges itself in my throat with the realization that Mom won't be there to make it better in the end. She's leaving us and the only thing I can do is give her this.

In that moment, I vow to do whatever it takes to get us out of this hellhole. It's up to me to save us from her fate.

"I promise, Momma." I jerk my head in a nod, tucking both my little brother and sister into my chest, pressing their little faces into me.

They miss the thug's machete as it comes down on our mother's neck, her eyes losing their light as soon as the blade connects with her body. In that moment I know, the sound of metal connecting with bone will forever be the prelude to my desolation.

As if in slow motion, Mom's head falls with a heavy thud. I should look away, but I can't. I'm transfixed by the horror, and my only tether to reality is the deep ache settling in my chest.

In complete contrast, the killer lets our mother drop to the floor, unaffected by his actions. His face devoid of emotion as he walks past the desecrated bodies of our parents, not even sparing us a glance as he leaves.

This can't be real. This can't be happening.

The fresh smell of copper creeps its way up my nose and I do my best not to gag at the vision before me.

This is very real. This is definitely happening.

"Shh. Don't look. Everything's going to be okay," I whisper to my brother and sister, my arms gripping tightly around their little bodies.

Even as I utter the words, I doubt their truth, but it's all I can offer. Words and a comforting embrace.

We have to get out of here.

My fingers stroke their greasy hair as I push us back toward the nearest wall, needing to get us as far from the horror show lying not two feet away.

Alex whimpers and I see that he's turned his head, his eyes locked onto our parents' lifeless bodies.

Damn it. I told him not to look.

Quickly pressing a hand to his eyes, I turn him toward me. No child should have to see their decapitated parents lying in a pool of their own blood.

I'm about to utter false words of hope when a thud outside has my grip tightening. *I know we're running out of time.* My mind races with ways of escaping whatever lies beyond that door, because deep in my bones, I know we won't last another night.

It's been a long week of starvation and beatings, ending with the death of our parents. There's no doubt we're next, and I can't let that happen.

Over my dead body.

A quick glance ahead lets me know… that just might be my future.

The door creaks open and my eyes focus on a man wearing full tactical gear. In all black, he looks like a dark angel and nothing like the men that have held us captive for far too long. *What's he doing here?*

He doesn't look like he wants to hurt us, but based on the fury rolling off of him in waves, I can tell he's capable of murder. With a string of curse words under his breath, the man finally turns, crouching in front of us.

"Hey, I'm Hudson," he whispers, holding both palms up. "I know this has been really hard for you, but we need to get you out of here before the bad guys return. You don't know me, but your uncle asked me and my friends to bring you home. Everything is going to be okay now."

I rear my head back, knowing that his words are the farthest thing from the truth. Things will never be okay again.

For fuck's sake, we just witnessed our mother lose her head next to Austin's lifeless body.

No. Things will never be okay.

Those words are just the same bullshit line I fed my little brother and sister. Only uttered to keep them calm.

"Look, the longer we stay here, the more dangerous it becomes for you. The men who did this..." he pauses, nodding toward the door behind him. "They'll be coming back any minute and we need to not be here when they do."

He's right. We need to get out of here, and fast. I lost track of how many armed goons came in and out of this room. Who's to say they don't have the numbers to stop our cavalry.

Closing my eyes, I take in a centering breath. *I can do this.* Even though I'm weary of any and all men, I'll be damned if I let my apprehension keep us from escaping.

Sending up a prayer, I hope that by some miracle, one of my uncles sent this man. My stomach churns as I quickly glance back at our mom. *It's either trust him or end up being next.*

Finally gathering the courage, I let him pull us up to standing.

"Okay. Stay behind me. My friends will help us get out of the compound, but we have to be fast and quiet. Can you do that for me?"

I give him a quick nod and grab a hold of Alex and Amanda's little hands, pulling them against me on either side.

This is it.

We either make it out of here alive... *or we don't.*

Chapter One

JACK

This cannot be happening… *Again*.

Pressing the heels of my palms to my eyes, I let the memories flood through me.

Four years to this day, we lost both of our parents at the hands of a bloodthirsty cartel. How sick and twisted is fate to have us now lose a brother to the very same assholes who ripped our family apart so long ago.

"Jack, are you listening?" My brother, Matthew, breaks me from the horror film replaying in my head.

"Yeah. I get it. It makes sense for the kids to come stay with me." I rub a hand over my face and let out a deep sigh.

"Hell yeah, it does," Jace, the youngest of five, chimes in. No doubt thrilled to have dodged the bullet of parenting. "You're the oldest, most established brother. Besides, you own tons of vacation properties so you'll have an endless supply of ways to keep the rug-rats entertained."

I roll my eyes. "They won't be here on an endless vacation, Jace. Kids need stability, not to be traipsing around from one property to another."

"You know what I mean. You have this massive ranch, with acres for them to play in. You also have the staff to step in when you're too busy with work." Jace cocks a brow, tilting his head toward Mary, who's dropping off a tray of drinks.

"Thank you, Mary. That'll be all." The matronly woman leaves my study with a small nod, her eyes swimming with pity.

Jace is right. My staff is like family, and that'll definitely come in handy when caring for two kids and a teenager. But even so, there's no compensating for my failures. How will I keep three damaged children when I couldn't even hold our family together after our own parents' death?

After the devastating news, each of the Crown brothers went their separate ways. Hell, it's a miracle we've stayed in touch at all these years.

"I'll agree to take on the kids if you'll agree to weekly video chats. There's no way in hell I'm doing this alone and I need to know that we are all in this together." I raise a brow, begging them to argue. I've been a shit brother, but if I'm doing this with the kids, then I'll have to give it my all. That means roping in the uncles.

Both men give me a tight-lipped nod.

Good.

"I'm not exactly jumping up to become daddy dearest, but

I'm only a couple of hours south if you or the kids need anything. Hell, even if it's just a breather. I'll watch them for the weekend." Matthew shoots me a sheepish smile, knowing full well he's just as capable of taking on the kids as I am.

"So, it's settled. You'll be their guardian." Jace lifts his drink, as if toasting to the resolution. "Matthew travels all the time because of work. I'm not equipped to care for myself, let alone kids." He's right about that, too. "And Hunter... Well, he'd just scare the shit out of the children."

I let out a deep chuckle at his last words. "That's for sure." Hunter is a through-and-through mountain man. He's always been brilliant, his mind preferring solitude to that of human company. It's why he's become a recluse, living up in the mountains and only touching base twice a year.

It's the reason he isn't here with us right now. He isn't even aware that we've lost Austin.

"Fuck. Who's going up there to tell him?" Matthew rubs at the back of his neck.

Since Hunter doesn't have a phone line, the only way of updating him would be to trek out to his cabin.

I lift my palms up. "Not it. I'm taking on parenting duties so it'll have to be one of you two knuckleheads."

"Fine." Jace scrunches his face as if he's smelled something foul. "It's the least I can do since I live the farthest away and won't be able to pop in like Uncle Matt here." He juts his chin out to Matthew.

I bring a tumbler of amber liquid to my lips, taking a long pull. "Speaking of which, have you given my offer any thought?"

Jace shakes his head vehemently. "Thanks, but no thanks. Why would I want to come work for you when I own one of the hottest nightclubs in Florida? Business is good, and I'd be a fool to throw that away."

Mathew sighs, "Because that environment is toxic, little bro. To be honest, I'm surprised you haven't knocked someone up or called us to bail you out."

"I'm not stupid, Matt. I wrap it up. No glove, no love." Jace states matter-of-factly.

I choke on my drink. "You *do* know that those things aren't one-hundred percent foolproof, right? There's always room for error. And lord knows the last thing you need is some VD or baby momma drama when I'm pretty sure you don't even know how to wipe your own ass."

"Ha. Fucking. Ha." Jace stands up, forcefully placing his rocks glass on my desk. "Laugh all you want. I'm the only Crown brother who's living it up. Meanwhile, y'all are slaves to your careers. When's the last time any of you got ass?"

I groan. Not even remembering the last time I dove into a woman's sweet warmth.

My staff is like family and there's no way I'd shit where I eat. Pair that with a lackluster night life and, well, it leaves for a very boring sex life.

"I can't speak for Jack, but I'm more than satisfied." The smug bastard takes a sip of his drink, his eyes glazing over, probably thinking of his latest conquest.

I crack my knuckles, needing to get our conversation back on track. "Are you two Casanovas going to stick around until drop-off? WRATH securities will be here tomorrow evening with the kids and I think it'd be best if they saw they have more family than just me waiting for them."

Both brothers nod before Jace speaks up, "Yeah, and then I'll head to Hunter's cabin on my way out."

"I'll have Mary take you to your rooms." Picking up the phone from my desk, I ring her office. "I'm sure y'all are tired from travel and stress. It's been one hell of a week."

They nod again, Matt rubbing at the scruff on his jaw. "Yeah. It sure has. And it's probably going to get crazier for you."

His brows raise. The implication of parenting struggles not lost on me.

My mind floats back to my brother, Austin. *Damn him.* We don't have all the details, but we do know that his family's abduction was no mere coincidence.

What the hell was he thinking getting involved with the Las Cruces Cartel?

Chapter Two

PENELOPE, AGE 8

Men. What are they even good for? For as long as I could remember, nothing. They're worthless. The first one to teach me this was Dad. He left Mom and me and never came back.

I don't know what he looked like but from what Mom has said, he was very handsome. But this one? He isn't even nice looking, with his noodle arms and bald head. He looks like Fester Adams.

"Penelope," Mom says in her serious voice. "Say hello to Charles."

"Hello, Charles," I droll, not willing to give this dude an ounce of excitement.

Charles looks nervously between mom and me. He probably didn't think a kid would be cramping their style.

Ha, Surprise!

"Hello, Penelope. That's such a pretty name." The corner of his mouth lifts upward in a smile, but I can tell that it's forced.

I don't respond. What's there to say?

Instead, I pickup my book, uninterested with whatever they've got planned for the next couple of hours.

My poor mom is a hopeless romantic. She believes in fairy tales and Prince Charming. Heck, she probably thinks Fester here is her forever love or that Santa and the Easter Bunny are real.

I let out a snort, realizing too late that Charles was staring at me expectantly.

Whoops.

Mom shoots me her death stare, complete with pursed lips. I guess she isn't happy with how I'm treating her latest boyfriend.

Too bad. This is all he's getting.

If he's like the others, I give him a month… *tops.*

Letting out a sigh of resignation, Mom pivots on her heels, her dark hair swishing as she gives me her back. In three quick strides, she speed-walks toward the television.

I know what she's doing, and it's not going to work.

The screen flits through various channels until she finally settles on a cartoon, thinking it'll keep me distracted.

Wrong. I hate cartoons. They're fake. Just like her fairytales. All full of fake laughs, fake friends, and fake families.

My eyes flit back to Charles, who's shifting his weight from left to right, unable to stand still.

"Alright, then." She shakes her head, landing her gaze on the eager man. "Shall we?" Mom extends an arm, showing him toward her room.

His half grimace, half smile turns into a full-on grin before he turns and starts walking toward the hallway.

Good riddance. The faster they get on with their date, the faster Mom will realize he's not the one. They never are.

I roll my eyes. Maybe one day she'll learn.

Men aren't the answer. They're the problem.

Penelope, Present Day

"You'll be staying with your uncle, Jack." The caseworker's voice jerks me out of my thoughts.

"I'm sorry. What did you say?" My brows push together, unsure if I heard her correctly.

"Jack. He's the uncle who hired the security team." She blinks once before looking back down at her file. "Yes." Her finger glides across the paper, the document no doubt confirming the terrible words she's uttered. "Your parents' wishes were that you'd remain with one of the Crown brothers should anything ever happen to them."

It's been twenty-four hours since we left Mexico, and my world is still spinning. All I know is that we're stateside and pending release based on our medical evaluations.

I'd finished my exam when this lady walked in claiming to be a social worker. Social worker my ass. She's more like the grim reaper of news.

She's just delivered a verbal blow that might as well have

been physical. There's no way I can stay with *him*.

My legs tuck underneath me, the movement making the paper on the exam table crinkle. "You said 'one of the Crown brothers,'" I chew on my bottom lip, trying to find a way out of this. "Why can't we stay with one of the other brothers? Matt? He's pretty stable."

"Jack is more than capable of caring for you and your siblings." Her eyes narrow as she reaches a hand to my shoulder. "That is unless there's something you haven't shared. Something that hasn't made its way onto our file."

My brows hit my hairline at her implication. "No. God, no." I quickly shake my head. Jack might be a Grade A asshole, but he's not a perv. Even though I can't stand him, there's no way I'd let him get labeled something he wasn't.

The social worker slides a business card onto my lap. "You know you can always call me if anyone steps out of line, right?"

I nod once, knowing beyond a shadow of a doubt that this won't ever be an issue.

Only fools repeat history, and I'm no fool.

Young naïve me, I let my crush-riddle heart fall for Jack Crown. He was older, wiser, and one hell of a flirt.

But I was his brother's stepdaughter and way too young. Definitely not someone he'd pay any mind.

Despite knowing fairytales were fake and that there's no such thing as happily ever after, I let myself trust this man. Let him get close enough to where I relied on his visits, his kind gestures, and what I thought was his love.

He was the male figure I looked up to, the only one I'd ever had. While Mom was busy with Austin, I had Jack.

Sure, I had to share him once Alex and Amanda were born, but I didn't mind. I was happy that they had his love too.

Stupid, naïve little girl.

Fate's a fickle bitch and, of course, she'd make it nice and clear that I was being dumb. Believing in things I had no right to.

What could a grown man want from a silly little girl and her siblings? No, I'm sure he had grown women to occupy his time.

One missed Sunday turned into two, and before I knew it, weeks turned into months, and months turned into years. Finally, on my fifteenth birthday, I locked away the last of my childish thoughts.

I was never on this man's radar. And if I can help it, I never will be.

Trees everywhere, as far as the eye can see. It really is stunning, and if I were anyone else, I'm sure I'd be gawking over the beauty.

We're on the road after having traveled on a private jet, the luxury a welcomed contrast from the hell we were forced to endure.

Still, I'd rather be anywhere but here.

"You ready to see your uncle Uncle Jack?" Ashley swivels her head, angling herself to face the rear seating of the luxury SUV. I have an entire row to myself, and my brother and sister are seated behind me.

We're being driven by Titus, one of the men on our rescue

mission, as well as his girl, Ashley. Despite her only being a couple of years older than me, she's managed to put on this mothering role and I want no part of it.

"He's not my uncle," I grumble while Alex and Amanda wordlessly stare out of their windows, continuing to ignore Ashley and the movie she's chosen to play on their built-in DVD players. Clearly, they want no part of her happy-go-lucky either.

Titus reaches over and squeezes Ashley's thigh in a comforting gesture. Right. Because she's the one that needs comforting.

Rolling my eyes, I attempt at niceties. "What I meant was, he's not my uncle anymore. Amanda and Alex are biologically tied to him through their dad, but I was only his niece through marriage. Now that our parents are…" I trail off, not wanting to finish that statement.

My chest tightens and my eyes burn. I will not cry. Not in front of the kids. Lord knows they're already traumatized as hell. They sure as fuck don't need their only source of strength breaking down in front of them.

Ashley gives me a sad smile. "Even so. He's still your guardian and I know he's excited to see you."

My lips press into a firm line, not trusting myself to speak.

I know for a fact that isn't true. If it were, he would've made more of an effort to see us over the last couple of years. But he didn't.

Alex, who's wise beyond his nine years, finally speaks up. "Pen is almost eighteen. Why can't we just stay at our house with her? She'll watch us."

I had this very conversation with the men of WRATH. To my dismay, they said I'd have to take it up with my uncles. More precisely, Jack.

Reaching back, I ruffle my little brother's hair. "I like the way you think, little man. But as much as I want to do that right now, I can't. It's still a couple of months until I turn eighteen and then I'd have to talk to Uncle Jack about it."

I leave out the part that our parents made their wishes abundantly clear. No need to tell the little ones that our parents had custody planned out in the event of their death, and it definitely wasn't leaving the kids to me.

My body shakes as I wrap both arms around myself. Did they know they'd leave us so soon?

The SUV comes to a full stop, breaking me out of my thoughts. We're here.

Whether or not I like it, this is home for the next couple of months. And despite how much I detest my uncle, I have to play nice.

Needing to convince him I'm capable of caring for my siblings will be the easy part. But preventing my hate from seeping through and tainting our chances will be nearly impossible.

With a deep inhale, I brace myself for what's to come. I only know one thing for sure—wherever I go, I'm taking the kids with me.

Chapter Three
PENELOPE

Wow. This place is *stunning*.

As soon as I step out of the SUV I'm confronted with a modern day farmhouse, outfitted in a white exterior with black accents and metal roof.

This place is massive. And when I say massive, I mean this place could double as a hotel.

Ashley sidles up to me. "This is the main house. From my understanding, all of the guests stay in the individual cabins scattered throughout the property."

I blink. So *this is* a hotel of sorts. Right about now I'm wishing I would've listened in on Austin's conversations about his brother. I have no clue what he's been up to these past years, and this information is definitely news to me.

A tiny hand slides into mine, and I look into the deepest shade of green. "Hey, pumpkin. I've got you."

I shoot my little sister a smile before pulling her forward and toward my dream home. Who'd've thought that my least favorite person would be the proud owner of my Pinterest perfect desire?

Looking at Alex, I give him a mischievous smirk. "This place is huge. Think you'll be able to find me in a game of hide and seek?"

His eyes light up before they dim again, clouded by the sadness that's been plaguing us since Mexico. "Dad was the best at hiding."

I reach down and pull him to my other side. "He sure was, buddy."

I'm still gripping onto both kids when the front double doors push open and a towering six-foot-three man steps through the frame.

My throat goes dry before I catch myself and clench my jaw. He may be a pretty shell with his lush black hair, chiseled jawline and bulging biceps—but that's all he is. A shell. All he cares about is where he'll dip his wick next. Why he's the one who ended up with us, I'll never know.

Based on what I've heard, Uncle Matt would've been a better fit for us. Not some manwhore who undoubtedly keeps a revolving door to his bed.

I'm about to give the man a paltry greeting when our eyes clash and my breathing halts. Something unrecognizable flashes behind his eyes, his nostrils flaring, before his brows push together. "Princess?" It comes out in a whisper before he clears his throat and tries again. "Pen?"

"The one and only." I raise a brow, keeping my grip on the kids. "You remember Alex, right? And this is Amanda. She would've been a year the last time you saw her."

The accusation in my tone is clear, but he seems unaffected. Ignoring my words, he crouches down in front of us.

"Hey Amanda and Alex. I know this isn't the same as your home, but I want you to know that I'll do whatever I can to make this place a happy one for you."

My heart squeezes. Not for the man, but for the kids. Regardless of my disdain for Jack, I still want what's best for the children. The fact that he sounds eager to make this as happy an experience as possible for them is comforting.

Jack rises to his full height, his eyes landing on Titus, completely bypassing me once more.

"Thank you for everything." He reaches out for Titus' hand, clapping another on his shoulder. "Our family will be indebted to you always."

"It's what we do. Hopefully, you'll never need our services again." Titus gives us all a sad smile as Ashley crouches down and hugs the kids.

She comes up to me next, sliding a card into my hand. "Call me." Ashley's eyes flit to Jack before coming back to mine again. "If you need *anything*. I mean it. That's my personal cell and I have it on me at all times."

I nod, giving her a small smile. She might be a little smothering, but I can see she has good intentions.

Ashley and Titus wave their final goodbyes as they load up into their SUV and pull out onto the drive.

This is it. This is really happening.

I'm staring after the disappearing SUV when the clearing of Jack's throat has me turning around, coming face to face with the stormiest hazel eyes I've ever seen. "Okay, then." He claps his hands together like some sort of camp counselor, though the look on his face is still grim. "Your things are being shipped from California, but I've set up some essentials in your rooms to hold you over until then. Let me know if there's anything I missed."

I meet his gaze, my mouth refusing to smile. "Thank you."

Jack gives one small nod. "Have y'all eaten? I'd ask if you're hungry, but if your appetite is anything like mine, I know it's non existent."

"The kids haven't had dinner yet." I suck in my lips and look ahead, avoiding his stupidly gorgeous face.

"Well, then it's a good thing Mary just finished fixing supper. She made her famous roast." He smiles at the kids while my stomach churns.

Mary... Is that his wife? Girlfriend? God, I really wish I'd paid more attention.

Things are already difficult as hell. Adding his latest romantic fling to the mix will only make it that much more awkward.

Whatever. I've got this. I'll put up with the devil himself if it means I'll be able to walk away from this with the kids.

I brace myself for what's to come as we all step through the front door, but what I see has me freezing in place. Two other Crown men are standing there, both with wide smiles on their faces.

My mouth hangs open as I take a step toward them. "Matt?

Jace?"

Before the men have had a chance to answer, Amanda and Alex quickly scurry behind me. The kids were never openly social and after last week's events, they've become skittish as hell.

Who can blame them?

"Hey, princess!" Jace walks toward me, pulling me into a hug.

Over his shoulder I can see Jack clenching his jaw, his narrowed gaze falling on his younger brother's arms. Deciding to ignore whatever's crawled up his butt, I focus my eyes on Uncle Jace.

"Hey!" I chuckle, definitely not having expected him to be here. He's the party animal out of the bunch and I'm sure there's a million things he'd rather be doing than attending a somber greeting. "This is a long way from South Beach. From what I've heard, this little town doesn't even have any nightclubs."

He releases me, pressing his hands to his heart. "You wound me! How could I miss out on seeing my favorite nieces and nephew?"

"But I thought I was the only nephew and you guys the only nieces." Alex looks between Amanda and me, making the entire room erupt in laughter.

I pat Jace on the shoulder. "You'll soon find that there isn't much you can get past Alex."

Jace ruffles Alex's hair while pulling on one of Amanda's pigtails. "I've got a special room set up for you guys. It's got video games, toys, and every imaginable lovie."

"He really did go overboard at the toy store the town over. I wouldn't be surprised if he did in fact have every imaginable lovie." Matt steps forward, leaning in for a side hug before bringing in both kids for the same.

Jack's gruff voice cuts in, "How about we let the kids eat first, then we'll all take them to the game room."

"Lead the way." Jace extends his hand toward the hallway, the wide corridor clad in white shiplap.

Damn, this place is gorgeous. All the ceilings are tall and each is finished with cathedral wood paneling.

We step into a formal dining room in all white and warm woods with enough seating to fit a football team.

"Sit wherever. Mary and Georgina will be out any second with the food." Jack takes a seat at the head of the table, the brothers sitting on either side of him.

My brows raise as I sit next to Jace. Mary *and* Georgina?

Alex sits next to Matt while Amanda takes the seat next to me. I'm scooting her chair in when an older woman with graying hair walks through one of the archways. "Dinner's here."

"Mary, you know I love your roasts." Matt rubs his hands together greedily, making me chuckle.

Jack speaks up, "Mary, thank you for dinner. I'm sure the kids will love every bite." He then turns to us, looking from right to left. "Kids, this is Mary. She manages the household. If there's anything you need, you go to her."

The kids nod, meanwhile I just stare on. Mary seems nice enough, but I can't rely on her if I want to prove that I can handle the kids on my own.

Jack's eyes narrow on mine while he addresses the matronly

woman. "Mary, do you mind sending Georgina out? She needs to meet the kids."

"Yes, sir. Of course." The woman steps around Matt, who's already giving himself healthy servings of the roast.

"Did I hear my name?" A beautiful young brunette steps from where I'm guessing the kitchen is, holding a casserole dish with mashed potatoes.

"Yes, Georgina. I wanted you to meet the kids." Jack waves a hand in our direction, the brunette blushing for some odd reason.

"Hello, children." She looks toward Alex and Amanda, giving them both warm smiles. "It's my job to keep the home tidy. And lucky me, I'll also be watching over you, making sure your rooms stay nice and neat."

Georgina completely ignores me, only giving me a passing glance. Okay?

"Thank you for that, but the kids have me to watch over them, and they can definitely straighten out their own rooms." I pin her with a glare. Who the fuck does she think she is, Mary Poppins?

Jace chokes on his water while Jack clears his throat. "Georgina, meet Penelope. The eldest of the kids."

Kids. He sees me as a kid. Well, if that isn't making a difficult situation seem nearly impossible. Looks like I have my work cut out for me.

Georgina presses her lips together in an attempt to prevent her lip from curling, but the disgust is clear on her face. What is her problem? Before I can ask, she gives me the fakest smile ever. "Nice to meet you, Miss Penelope."

I just sigh. *Fuck her*. She clearly doesn't like me, and I don't have time for fake bullshit.

I've seen how cruel and unforgiving life can be. The time we have is fleeting and I'm not wasting a damn second on appeasing this fake ass bitch.

FILTHY CROWN

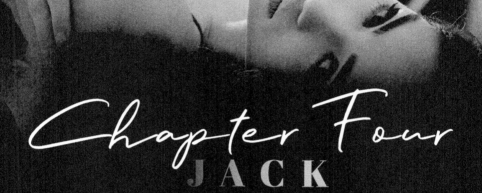

Chapter Four

JACK

"**S**eems like you're going to have your hands full with Pen," Matt mumbles into his whiskey.

Jace snorts. "That's an understatement if I ever heard one."

The kids are now settled in their rooms and we're in my den; the fire roaring as we all sit and sip our after-dinner drinks, all of us having opted for Matt's private label, Tortured Crown whiskey. I let out a long sigh. To say that introductions with the staff went smoothly would be a lie. "I didn't expect rainbows and sunshine, but hell, I thought with Pen being the oldest she'd be the easiest."

Matt nearly spits his drink out. "A teenage girl? Easy? Man, are you out of touch with reality."

I rub a hand over my face and sigh. "I guess so, brother. It's just... the Pen I remember was so easygoing and happy. This Pen... She's like a whole new person." I groan, taking a long pull from my drink. "Hell, I didn't even recognize her when she stepped out of the car. Thought she was someone with WRATH securities."

I'd watched her long tanned legs step toward me, her dark brown hair flowing in waves down her back. *She was stunning. She is stunning.*

Not that my little princess wasn't beautiful before. But she was just that. Little. With long lanky legs and a mouth full of braces, she was nothing more than my brother's stepdaughter. A child.

But the girl sleeping upstairs resembles anything but a child. With her soft curves and full lips, the thoughts she elicits are all full grown.

My cock twitches, and I huff out a breath. *Fuck, I'm screwed.* I know I shouldn't be thinking of her like this. It's wrong. More than wrong. It's illegal. She's underage, and my niece for fuck's sake.

Maybe a night out in the next town over will help push these sinful thoughts out of my head.

"So, Matt. Are you still up for babysitting?"

"Ha! It hasn't even been one night and you're already wanting out of parenting duties?" Matt shakes his head. "Anyway, I'm up for next weekend, though I think they'd probably benefit from stability."

"That's what I'm thinking too. That's why you can come stay here during your time with them."

Jace claps his hands together. "Hey, I can get in on the

babysitting action, too. A weekend with Uncle Jace."

"No!" Matt and I both shout in unison.

Jace holds his hands up in surrender. "Fine. Fine. Message received."

"Good. Now that we have that out of the way, what's your plan for getting to Hunter's cabin?"

"I'm taking one of your trucks and driving up after breakfast tomorrow. The weather should be mild enough as we enter into the summer with the snow mostly gone."

The ranch is located down valley, but Hunter's cabin is an hour north on Bell Mountain. "Be careful. You know the roads aren't fully clear until the dead of summer."

"Ten-four, big bro. I'll take two of the satellite phones with me and leave one up there with Hunter. There's no way I'm letting him off the hook. If I'm forced to do weekly check-ins, then so is he."

Matt grumbles, "It shouldn't be a hardship to talk with your nieces and nephews, Jace."

"Hey, that's not what I meant. I love the kids. I'm just not a routine kind of guy. I'm more of a free spirit." Jace lifts his drink, swaying it side to side.

Matt and I both groan. "Speaking of spirits, which one possessed Austin? It's not like he didn't know who he was getting into bed with. We've had our suspicions for a while now, and I think it's safe to say that Las Cruces cartel is the number one suspect in our parents' murder."

Matt's hand grips tightly around his rocks glass. "I think it's time we brought WRATH securities in on this. We've been living with this for far too long, and with all of us going our separate ways, it's been left to the wayside."

Jace puts his drink down, lifting both palms toward us in supplication. "Whoa, whoa, whoa. I thought we left it behind us because that's where it belongs. Dealing with local assholes is one thing, but this is a massive blood thirsty cartel." He stands, pacing in front of us. "If our parents wanted to do business with them, they should have known what they were getting into. Same goes with Austin."

There's venom in my little brother's words. A deep-rooted anger I rarely see in him has taken him over.

"Sit down, Jace. Nobody is going knocking on the cartel's door." Matt shakes his head, but I see what's really bothering our little brother.

I stand and head over to him, placing an anchoring hand on his shoulder. "I get it. They left us here to pick up their messes. Their selfish actions didn't take into account how those around them would be affected."

Jace gives a jerky nod, his lips rolling into a firm line.

Keeping my eyes on him, I continue. "But we're not selfish. Our hearts won't allow us to move forward without holding those responsible for their deaths accountable. Right?"

Jace falls back into his seat with a whoosh. "Shit. Why do you always have to make sense?"

"I don't, but I'm glad you think so." I walk back to my chair, before looking at both of my brothers. "Are we doing this, then? Hiring the men of WRATH securities to look into this for us?"

"Fine. But just so you know, if one of you goes missing, I'm not sending in for a rescue." Jace smirks before picking up his glass and taking a sip.

34

I shake my head and laugh. "Sure thing, brother. Sure thing."

Coffee. I'm in desperate need of coffee.

Rubbing my temples, I shuffle into the kitchen as the sun begins to rise, its rays illuminating the space with a warm glow.

Success. Mary started a pot. I'm about to pull down a mug when a groan has me spinning around.

"Fuck. Fuck. Fuuuuuck." Pen is staring at a laptop screen, her brows pushed together and lips turned down into a scowl.

"Pen? What are you doing up so early?" It's five in the morning and I'm usually the only soul moving around at this hour.

Her honey-colored eyes meet mine and it's like I'm zapped with a current of energy.

"Mary let me borrow a laptop. It's been over a week since I checked my portfolio and everything went to shit since I was gone." She grimaces as if catching herself.

I feel my brows raise. "Portfolio? As in…"

She sighs, bringing both hands to her face before her fingers swipe up into her scalp. "Stocks. I day trade."

"But you're seventeen. Don't you need to be an adult before you get an account with a brokerage firm?"

She raises a brow, clearly not amused. "I have an account under the UTM Act. Technically, Austin was supposed to be the one trading on my behalf, but he pretty much gave me free range."

"Wow." I just stand there holding my empty mug because,

holy fuck. Here she is at seventeen, making serious money moves when all I cared about at her age was getting laid.

"Yeah. I'm supposed to gain full control in three months when I turn eighteen."

I nod. "Does his... being gone, affect the account at all?"

Her little shoulders rise up in a shrug. "I figure as long as the transfer happens before the estate is closed out, I should be fine."

I slowly nod, trying to make sense of everything she's just dropped on me. "Okay. Well, I'm the one handling the estate, so I'll look into that for you."

She blows out a breath before getting up and heading toward the fridge. She's wearing tiny sleep shorts, her round cheeks peeking out of the bottom with each step she takes.

Fuck. I swivel my head so fast, I practically give myself whiplash.

I cannot be looking at her ass.

"Thank you," her voice comes out so small it has me turning back, my brows dropping and eyes narrowing.

"There's no need to thank me. We're family. It's what we do." Family. That's right, you sick fuck. She's family.

"But are we, though?" She takes out a tall glass filled with dark liquid and fills it with ice. *Is that coffee?* "Now that Austin is gone, we aren't exactly tied together. I'm surprised you even agreed to take me in."

My head rears back as if slapped. "What the hell? I would never turn you away, Pen. How could you even think that?"

She pours milk into the cup, her lip curling back in a sneer. "Gee, maybe because you abandoned me four years ago?"

What. The. Fuck.

"Pen, I—"

A shrill scream cuts through the house, both of our heads swinging toward the sound.

Before I can ask what the hell is happening, Pen drops her glass and runs out of the room. "Amanda! I'm coming, baby!"

I quickly follow, my mind racing with all possible scenarios. *Did she fall? Is she hurt?*

God, it hasn't even been twenty-four hours and I'm already a shitty guardian. Maybe they should have gone to Matt instead.

Chapter Five

PENELOPE

*D*amn. I knew this was going to happen. You can't walk away from seeing a decapitated body and come out unscathed. It's too much for a little mind to bear.

I'm flying, taking two steps at a time before coming to a complete halt outside Amanda's door. There, sitting up on her bed, is my little sister. Her gold locks clinging to her sweat slicked face and neck as she pushes away from Georgina.

"Get the fuck away from her!" I growl, flinging myself toward my sister and pulling her into a protective embrace.

"I–I–I was just trying to help." She gets up from the bed, wringing her hands on her too skimpy nightgown. *What the hell?* She's dressed like she's ready to walk down the Victoria Secret runway. "I heard her scream, so I rushed inside to see what happened. She was hysterical when I found her, but she wouldn't let me calm her."

I stare at her incredulously. Of course she wouldn't let her calm her. She doesn't even know her. Flicking my gaze toward Jack, I see he's just standing there as if on mute. If he won't say something, I sure will.

"Keep your hands to your damn self, Georgina. It'd be clear to a blind man that you're only making things worse." I stroke the palm of my hand down Amanda's back, trying to stop her from sobbing. "Shh. I've got you, pumpkin. You're safe here."

Georgina rushes to Jack's side, her hands lifting to his chest. "I was just trying to help, Jack. I want you to know that I'm here for you. I'll always be here for you and the kids."

I look away, unable to withstand one second longer of this woman flinging herself at Jack like some desperate floozy.

Amanda whimpers, "Pen. Don't leave me."

God. My heart.

Out of the corner of my eye, I see Jack clench and unclench his fists. "Georgina, why don't you go put some clothes on. We've got this covered." The hulking man approaches us slowly before crouching down next to the bed. "Amanda, I promise you're safe here. Nothing and nobody can hurt you. Uncle Jack's got you."

She gives him a weary glance. *Justifiably so.* With no recollection of him aside from yesterday's interaction, I'm surprised she's let him come this close.

"What happened, sweetie? Was it a bad dream?" I pull back, trying to see her face clearly.

Not liking the distance, she reaches for me, pressing her little sweat covered face into my shirt. "The men. They came back for you. They took you, too."

Jesus. I cling to her, desperately trying to give her comfort. "I'm here. I'm not going anywhere. Promise."

My sister sobs, her tears soaking the fabric between us. "You can't promise, Pen. Mom promised, and she left."

Jack sucks in a sharp breath, his tortured eyes meeting mine in a helpless clash. "Well, Pen has me and I'll do everything in my power to make sure this promise is kept." He raises a hand, tightly rubbing at the back of his neck. "I know it's going to take time to see that I'm telling the truth, but in the meantime, is there something that would help you feel better?"

Amanda looks at me then back at Jack, her glassy eyes lighting up a little. "Chocolate chip pancakes?"

Jack and I let out a chuckle at the unexpected request. I bop her nose, and smile. "Pancakes sound perfect. I think I saw what we needed when I was down in the kitchen earlier." Looking toward our guardian, I give him a lopsided smile. "How about it, Uncle Jack? You up for flipping duty?"

"Sure am. Come on, peanut. I'll sneak you some chocolate chips before we dump them in the batter." He extends a hand out to Amanda, and to my surprise, she takes it.

Maybe the stay here won't be too bad.

I'm mixing the batter when the rest of the crown brothers, sans Hunter, walk in.

"Something smells good in here." Matt rubs his belly and

looks toward the bacon sizzling on the skillet.

"Uncle Jack is making me pancakes." Amanda claps her little hands excitedly.

I bring a hand to my chest and give an exaggerated gasp. "So, what am I? Chopped liver?"

In all honesty, I'm happy she's taking a liking to Jack. I worried she wouldn't be able to recover from her trauma, but seeing that she's willing to accept a male figure in her life is promising.

"I wouldn't say chopped liver. More like prickly cactus fruit." Alex walks into the kitchen rubbing his eyes, the entire room erupting into laughter at his comment. Well, everyone except for me.

I scoff. "Fine. Don't expect to get any pancakes then."

"Don't worry. I'll give you some of mine," Amanda whispers conspiratorially.

"I see how it is." Smirking, I plop the batter down next to Jack, who's flipping the bacon.

His towering frame leans toward me, his lips a mere breath away from my ear. "Hey, why don't you go change? Your shorts are awfully short."

My face grows hot and my chest tightens. Slowly, oh so slowly, I turn to look him in the eye. "Excuse me?"

I must have heard him wrong, because he did not tell me my shorts are too short when Little Miss Sunshine was just prancing around like some goddamn lingerie model not thirty minutes ago. Besides, we're all family here, right?

"Everything okay over there?" Matt raises a brow in our direction while Jace pours himself a cup of coffee.

Jack's jaw clenches, his eyes narrowing into tiny slits, his gaze never leaving mine. "Fine. I was just telling Pen that she needs to go change into something more appropriate for company."

Oh. My. God. How freaking embarrassing!

Jace spits out the coffee he'd just sipped and Matt's brows practically hit his hairline. Meanwhile, I'm pretty sure I resemble a damn tomato.

"Brother, nobody is looking at Pen in any way, shape or form, that would warrant that kind of worry." Matt's brows furrow as his gaze flicks between me and Jack.

Something flashes in Jack's eyes, but he quickly schools his face into one of indifference before turning back toward his brother. "We have the therapist coming today and she needs to get checked out by the doctor."

My head whips toward him. "You didn't tell me the therapist was coming today?"

Amanda quickly scurries over to me, her arms wrapping around my legs. I look down, wondering if they'll be able to help with her nightmares.

"I don't want a therapist." Alex cuts into my thoughts as he calls from behind a cup of orange juice.

I let out a slow breath. This isn't going to be easy. "I know you're really strong, Alex. But can you do it as a favor for me? I'm sure it'll help your sister feel more comfortable with the idea."

He looks down at his little sister and nods. "Fine. For Amanda."

Thank God. He really is strong, but I know he's just as messed up about this as Amanda and me. It simply isn't natural. You can't see the kind of carnage we did and be okay.

Hell, I know I'm not, and I'm almost eight years older than him.

Jace walks toward me, handing me a cup of coffee. "Here. Looks like you've earned it." His soft smile melts my heart, bringing me back to the here and now.

"Thank you." I place the mug on the counter before depositing Amanda on one of the stools. They're shaped like saddles and she squeals at the realization.

"This is fun! Do you have real horsies?" She beams up toward Jack expectantly.

"We sure do. Maybe we can go for a ride after your therapy session." Jack is talking to Amanda, but his eyes are narrowed on me as I place the mug Jace gave me into the fridge. "You're putting your coffee... into the fridge."

"Yes, Captain Obvious. I don't like hot drinks, so I take my caffeine ice cold."

"Like your heart," Alex snickers, my eyes cutting to him and narrowing before they flit back to Jack, who's making a face of disgust.

"That's just wrong. It's sacrilege."

"Well, good thing it's not you who's drinking it, but me." I purse my lips and head back toward the stools, taking the one next to Amanda.

"Shouldn't you be going upstairs to change instead of desecrating coffee?"

My head rears back, my tongue poised to say something when Jace smacks Jack on the back. "Careful, brother. The way you two bicker, it might give someone the wrong impression."

For the second time, my face heats while Jack scoffs. "Like what? I'm just worried about what she's putting in that mouth."

It's Matt's turn to choke on his coffee as my eyes go wide. "Right. Well, on that note... I'm taking Amanda and Alex upstairs so we can all change for the day. We'll be right back."

I get up from my stool as Jace shoos us away. "Yes. Go before this one puts his whole leg in his mouth."

"Coffee. I was talking about her cold coffee." I hear Jack mutter as I step into the hall.

God. It's barely day two and things are not going well with Jack. Nothing I do seems to be good enough in his eyes. How in the world am I going to convince him I can manage things on my own?

Chapter Six
JACK

"What was that about?" Matt peers at me while sneaking a piece of bacon.

"What do you mean?" I look at him as if he's speaking a different language, unwilling to address the elephant in the room.

He shoots me a raised brow. "The whole 'I'm just worried about what she's putting in that mouth.'"

Visions of my fat cock sliding in and out of Pen's full lips slam into me, causing my knees to go weak and making them buckle.

Sucking in a ragged breath, I try to play it off. "I'm just taking this parenting role seriously. I didn't ask to be their surrogate dad, but now that I have the job, I'll be damned if I fail at it."

Matt raises a brow. "And iced coffee has what role in this?"

"Seriously," Jace chimes in, slapping me on the back. "The

way you were going at her, it didn't seem fatherly. It was more tyrannical than anything."

Matt snorts. "If that's what you want to call it. If I had to place a label on it, I'd say it was possessive with a touch of controlling."

"Tyrannical. Fatherly. Aren't they the same thing?" I quip, choosing to ignore Matt's input and instead think back to how our dad was with us growing up.

"Yeah, if you want her to hate you." Jace shudders. "You can thank Dad for my free spirit ways. Had he not been the hard ass he was, I think I would have ended up in a suit somewhere up in a high-rise." He shakes his head before taking a sip of his coffee. "Hell, maybe you're onto something with your harping."

"Shit. I'm fucking this up already, aren't I?" I run a hand through my hair, tugging at the ends.

"Hey, it's not like you got years of parenting under your belt before having to deal with a teenager. Give yourself a break. You gained instant dad status to three kids with none of the experience or preparation that comes with it." Matt's words have the knot in my stomach loosening a bit.

"Just think. You can't fuck 'em up worse than what they saw in Mexico," Jace contributes, his words making me cringe.

"Speaking of which, I'm glad the therapist is coming today. Amanda had a nightmare last night, Alex seems to be acting like nothing happened which isn't normal, and Pen…" I trail off. There's so much going on there I don't even know where to start.

"I looked over the report." Matt's brows push together, his

nostrils flaring. "It doesn't look like they… touched her."

"I saw that too." I let out a low rumble, not even wanting to think of someone touching her that way. The thought makes my blood boil, and I'm not sure if the reasoning behind it is entirely paternal.

Jace's brows shoot up. "That's a little strange, right? I mean, don't get me wrong. I'm glad they didn't. More than glad. But Pen is a knockout, and she was held by a damn cartel. They aren't exactly the pinnacle of morality."

"Do you think she could've lied to the medics who checked her over?" Matt looks between Jace and me before landing on the kitchen entryway. "I've heard of victims not wanting to admit to it."

A violent shudder shakes me where I stand, my hands gripping tightly onto the edge of the kitchen counter. "God, I pray that isn't the case." A cloud of red hazes my vision while scenes of me storming some cartel stronghold come to mind. I'm ripping off the balls of any man that touched her, even if it's the last thing I do.

"Pray that what isn't the case?" Pen looks between my brothers and me, her eyes narrowed into tiny slits as if she knows we were just talking about her.

My eyes take her in. She's wearing a black spaghetti strap dress that hugs all of her curves, the hem hitting her mid thigh. As if the dress wasn't tempting enough, tanned legs stem out and pour into combat style boots. The whole look is edgy yet soft.

I make a mental note to talk to Mary. What was she thinking, buying this type of clothing for her?

Like a freight train pulling the brakes too late, the wrong words pour out of me. "Is that what you're wearing?"

She cocks her head back, her mouth parting slightly before she snaps it shut again.

"Jack?" Matt warns, his tone teasing.

My jaw clenches, unsure of what to say. I'm not backing off. The therapist is a man and I'll be damned if I let him see her like this. "Stay out of this, Matt. I'm her guardian. I know what's best, and that's putting some more goddamn clothes on."

"It's okay Uncle Matt," she answers him but shoots me a lethal glare as she saunters over to the table, picking up a flannel button-up I'd left there the night before. She puts it on over her dress, rolling up the sleeves and leaving it open in the front like an oversized cardigan. I approve of the additional clothes, but her next words rock me to my core.

"Jack is just being a good..." with a bat of her lashes and a lick of her lips, she releases the one word that has me practically coming in my pants, "Daddy."

Fuck. Hearing that word fall from her pouty lips has blood flooding south, my cock hardening in an instant. Not good. This is not good.

Jace chokes on a piece of bacon while Matt smacks his back forcefully.

There's no doubt in my mind she's teasing me. Why? I have no fucking clue. But this shit can't continue. I need to reign in my bodily reactions, and she needs to realize that I only want what's best for her.

"Where are the kids, Pen?" My jaw ticks as I try to temper my emotions.

"Why? Going to scold them about their choice of apparel?" She closes her eyes and takes in a deep breath. But when she snaps them open, a blank look replaces the irritated one she'd just had moments ago. "I'm sorry. They're in the playroom. Alex is reading a book and Amanda is watching a cartoon. I was coming in here to ask if you had a baby monitor. Yes, I know they're older, but the house is big and they have been through so much. I'd like to keep an eye on them at all times if possible."

Who the fuck is this woman and what did she do to teenager Pen? She just went from sassy teenager to responsible woman in two seconds flat.

I'm standing there blinking like a dumbass when Jace speaks up, "The house is wired in all of the main areas. You can login and see the cameras if you have access to a smartphone or tablet."

Pen nods. "I think I can make that work. I lost my phone in Mexico, but I have the laptop Mary let me borrow, so I bet I can log in through there."

Crap. Something else I've let fall through the cracks. "You don't have to do that. I'll get you a phone and your own laptop. You'll need both for when you go off to college."

Pen stills. "About that." She nervously chews on her bottom lip, the action making me restless with need. Well, until her words hit me like an ice-cold bucket. "I'm not going to college."

Oh, hell no. She's got three months before she turns eighteen. Three months before the fall semester starts. And based on what the social worker told me, she'd been accepted into an ivy league school on a full ride. Not that she needs it. She's getting her trust fund as soon as she's of age.

That's one thing Austin did right. Made sure the kids were set up financially if anything were to ever happen to him.

"And on that note, I'll be heading out." Jace stands, Matt following his lead. "This is a conversation for Daddy. You know, since you're the guardian and you know best."

The bastard has the balls to snicker as he picks out keys for one of the ranch trucks.

Matt sidles up to him. "If you don't mind, brother. I think I'll tag along. It's been a minute since we've seen Hunter and I want to be there when he gets the news."

The tension in the room evaporates, replaced with sadness. The reality of our situation is heavy, outweighing whatever parenting was about to take place. With a sigh, I look over at Penelope. "This conversation isn't over. In the meantime, head to the playroom and take the laptop with you. I'll come get you when the therapist arrives."

Pen blinks, those ever-changing hazel eyes going glassy. "Are you dismissing me?"

"No, Princess." The old term of endearment flows easily from my lips. "I just need to talk to the guys before they leave, and I'd also like to discuss a couple of things with the therapist before you all see him."

She gives me a curt nod, but her expression is unreadable. Before I can ask if she's okay, she's waving goodbye to Matt and Jace, her long, dark hair swinging as she whips around and books it out of the kitchen.

Jace places his hand on my shoulder. "I don't envy you, brother. Dealing with teenage attitude is no joke, but try to be a little less Stalin and a little more Gandhi."

Matt's eyes narrow. "Are you going to be okay, Jack?"

"Am I? I have no damn clue. But I owe it to the kids to try. I owe it to Austin and Blanca, too." Rolling in my lips, I pinch them between my teeth.

"I'm talking about Pen's flirty sass, brother." Matt's brows push together, the tension clear on his face. "I know you'd never cross that line with her. She's a kid, for fuck's sake. But anyone from the outside looking in could see it differently. She could end up getting you into trouble."

What Matt's saying makes sense, but the thought of Pen leaving this ranch has my blood running cold. "No. She stays here. Besides, she only has three months left until she's eighteen and off to college."

Jace gives me side eye. "So you're going to pretend like she didn't just straight up shoot that idea down?"

I stiffen at his words. "Like I said. I'm the guardian and I know what's best. She's going to college, and that's that."

"Yes, Daddy." Jace bats his lashes in mock adoration, earning him a shove from Matt.

"Stop. He's already getting shit from a damaged teenager. He doesn't need it from you too."

I shake my head and laugh. "Enough of that." I pull a cupboard open, moving things around until I find what I need. "Here, take the satellite phones and call me after you've broken the news to Hunter. I'd like to talk to him too. Maybe get him to move down a little closer."

"Ha! Fat chance of that happening." Jace swipes the phones before he gives me a one-armed hug. "But there's always hoping."

Matt gets in on the hug action before we all break apart and I walk them to the door, feeling the need to warn them. "Stay safe, brothers. Lord knows this family can't survive another tragedy."

They both hum in agreement before trotting down the porch and toward the barn housing the trucks. Shifting my gaze toward the sky, I send out a silent prayer to the powers that be. For protection, patience, and a *shit ton* of willpower.

FILTHY CROWN

Chapter Seven

PENELOPE

Damaged teenager.

Matt's words keep replaying in my head. Over and over again, like a record on loop. I know I shouldn't've eavesdropped, but I wanted to know what was so important that I had to leave the room.

Serves me right, I guess.

Agh! I want to scream! I'm trying my hardest to show Jack that I'm responsible and that I'll be able to take on the kids when I turn eighteen, but no matter what I do, I end up bickering with the man.

I knew better than to sass him, but I couldn't help it. He drives me absolutely berserk.

Clutching the laptop to my chest, I remember the look in his

My mind flits back to the way his body tensed and jaw clenched. There's no denying that my words affected him.

He liked it. Damn. Who am I kidding? I liked it too.

But still, that was definitely the wrong move. No matter how much I want to get under his skin—annoy the hell out of him and hurt him the way he did me—I can't. Not if I want to make good on my promise to Mom.

I let out a frustrated sigh as I push the door to the playroom open. Thank god Alex and Amanda are good kids. I don't know how I'd navigate this if they were little carbon copies of me.

"Pen!" Alex looks up from his book while Amanda rushes for my legs.

"Hey, tiny terrors." The term of endearment is clearly facetious, but it makes them giggle just the same. "Y'all ready for the therapist? Uncle Jack said he'd be here soon."

Amanda just nods, but Alex scrunches up his face. "Do I have to? I really don't want to. I'm fine."

Blinking, I try to swallow my immediate reaction. How can anyone be fine after what we went through?

Despite my apprehension with strangers, maybe this therapist can tell us why Alex thinks he's fine.

I pick up Amanda and walk over to the couch, plopping us down next to our brother. "You're strong, buddy. But you, me, and Amanda just went through a lot. Saw a lot of stuff that leaves darkness and hurt buried inside us. And And that darkness can make our hearts sick without us even knowing it. That's why this is so important. Sometimes the only way we can find it and let it heal is by talking about it."

"But what if I don't want to find it? What if I want to leave that darkness alone?" His eyes search mine, trying to find a solace I don't even have.

Reaching for his little hand, I give it a squeeze. "Sometimes we have to do hard things, things that aren't so fun, because they're what's good for us."

"Like eating broccoli?" Amanda's tiny voice cuts in, making me chuckle.

"Yes. Like eating broccoli."

"Well, I'll eat all the broccoli in the world if it means I don't have to talk to the therapist." Alex looks at me, his statement in earnest.

"Ha! If only life worked that way. Gosh, imagine. I don't want to clean my room, so I'll eat a plate of broccoli instead. And *poof!* A clean room magically appears." I'm shaking my head and smiling big when the door creaks open, breaking our conversation.

A towering Jack walks in with his jaw ticking and broad shoulders practically taking up the entire door frame. It's not until he moves aside that I see the man behind him. "Kids, meet Dr. Leventhal."

The therapist seems to be in his forties, with a similar build to Jack and wisps of grey touching his temples. He's not as tall as our uncle, but he's no shrimp. What is it with Colorado men? Is there something in the water?

"Hello, Dr. Leventhal," I greet, squeezing both kids' hands and urging them to do the same, which they do.

"Hello, children. It's nice to meet you, although I wish it were under better circumstances." A small frown touches his lips before he catches himself, giving us a fake smile. "If you're all okay with it, I'd like to talk to everyone in this room. We can start with Alex, and then Amanda, once my colleague comes inside. She's a play therapist and I find it's easier sometimes when we talk through play."

I nod, thinking that's a good idea. Nonetheless, I get up and walk toward the laptop I'd dropped when I first walked in. This man is crazy if he thinks he'll be unsupervised during his visits. I don't care what letters follow his name.

Looking toward the kids, I give them an encouraging smile. "I won't be too far, and this room is wired with cameras. So just call out my name if you need me. I'll be able to hear you and come right on in."

I glance at the therapist, making sure my words are loud enough for him to hear me, not caring if I hurt his feelings. I want him to know that he's being watched.

He gives me a genuine smile; the action making me feel a little better about having Alex start first. He seems to understand and isn't threatened by the surveillance.

Dr. Leventhal looks away and toward my brother. "Alex, shall we begin?"

"I'd rather eat broccoli, but I guess I have to." Alex puts down his book and looks up at the doctor expectantly.

I know I should walk out, but my feet are firmly on the ground, as if weighed down by concrete. That is, until a strong hand falls to my lower back, the touch sending warmth through my body.

Jack leans in, his lips brushing against the shell of my ear. "Let him work."

With a soft tug of my hips, Jack steers me out of the

playroom, a curious Amanda in tow. "Can I stay with Alex? I want to play too."

Her pout is too damn cute, the move making me chuckle. "It'll be your turn soon. We're just waiting on the play therapist."

I shoot Jack a questioning glance and he nods. "Yes. She was just getting some things from their car. We're quite the drive from the airport."

"Airport? They aren't local?" My brows push together, wondering why on earth we wouldn't have gone with someone a little closer.

"No. They're from Dallas. The best, and they come highly recommended by a family friend." He doesn't even bat a lash as if it's the most normal thing in the world to fly in doctors for every visit.

"Um, that sounds pretty damn expensive. I'm sure we could find a good doctor whose invoice won't include airfare." I raise a brow, trying to knock some sense into the man. *See?* I can be a conscientious adult.

Jack stops in his tracks, making Amanda's small frame run into me. He slowly turns, boring his eyes into mine and with calloused fingers, he cups my cheek. "Pen, I'd give up every cent I own if it'd make you whole."

My chest tightens and eyes prickle. That can't be right. He can't care that much. If he did, then why did he leave me?

Jack's eyes narrow, his whiskey-colored orbs flitting back and forth between mine. The intensity in his gaze is too much. His words are too much.

Blinking tears away, I break away from his touch and walk

right past him, dragging Amanda's hand in mine. "We'll be in the kitchen if you need us."

Without another glance back, I leave him in the hallway. I have no idea what he's thinking, saying things he doesn't mean, stirring up feelings he has no right to.

He's a deserter. Just like my father and every other man that's come into my life thereafter. I'd be a fool to let myself fall for his words, and I'm no fool.

I need space. Space from this man that has my chest feeling all funny and my head not thinking clearly.

Unfortunately for me, I've barely made it into the kitchen when Jack's thick fingers wrap around my wrist and pull me into his chest. He dips his chin, his eyes staring into mine while he speaks into the room. "Amanda, can you go into the pantry and find the cookie mix?"

"Uh-huh!" Amanda claps her hands excitedly and walks off into the butler's pantry just as Jack walks me back into the wall, his grip on my arm punishing.

His body is flushed with mine, the rise and fall of his chest pushing against my breasts with every breath.

"Now listen here, little girl. I don't know what ideas you have floating around in your head, but I care about you. I've always cared about you." His jaw clenches and nostrils flare. "This isn't the time or place, but we'll be talking about this. *Soon.*"

The pitter patter of little feet scurrying toward us has him releasing his grip, but not before he dips his head and runs his nose along my jawline, inhaling my scent.

Holy shit. I think my panties are soaked.

Damnit. No! He's not making me fall again. I won't survive it. The last time he broke me, I was a naïve little girl, and it was nothing more than puppy love. *Now*? Now, he's dragging lust into the mix. An emotion I wasn't capable of feeling back then, but sure as hell am now.

I shoot him a glare. Unwilling to let him know just how much he affects me. Despite what his lips spew, his actions speak the truth. Those actions proved I was nothing more than a blip in his memory. And it'd serve me well to remember that.

Penelope, Fifteen Years Old

Another Sunday. Another letdown.

I'm sitting by the window waiting–*I'm always waiting*–but he never comes.

It's been two years since he stepped foot in our home, breaking our weekly tradition.

Is it me? Did I do something wrong? Did I make him mad?

My chest aches, and my stomach feels heavy and sick. I blow out a slow breath as I play with a loose thread on my sparkly party dress. I wore it for him. It's his favorite color. Blue.

Now I hate blue.

This is why I told mom fairytales are for children. They make you believe in dumb things that aren't real. There's no happily ever after.

The only ones on to something were the Brothers Grimm. Their stuff has truth in it. That witch lulling children into her candy cottage, only for her to turn around and eat them? Yeah, that's what men are.

Just like my father. They're supposed to be there for you, but when it matters, when it really matters, they're not. They leave you all alone with this sick hurt in your chest.

Jack is no different. Like the witch in the woods, he lulled me into thinking he'd always be there. For five years, he'd always come to my recitals and bring me flowers. He'd take me for milkshakes, listening to me talk about stupid boys and mean girls.

But it was all a lie. He did worse than eat me alive. He broke my heart. Tore apart the last bit of faith I had in men.

My nose stings as I swallow the lump in my throat. *I've been so stupid.*

Today is my birthday, and the wish I made as I blew out the candles? I wasted it on Jack. I wished that he would come, surprising me like he used to. I didn't care about presents or money. All I wanted was Jack.

My heart sinks as I search the driveway one last time, a lone tear trickling down my face.

It's time. Time that I put aside childish things like fairytales, love, and men.

Actions don't lie, and I've known the truth since my dad walked out. I should have known better.

Being foolish and stupid, I clung to childish thoughts. But no more. No. Men are worthless, and all they do is leave.

As I turn, abandoning my post at the window for the very last time, I vow to never let them trick me again.

I'm better off alone.

FILTHY CROWN

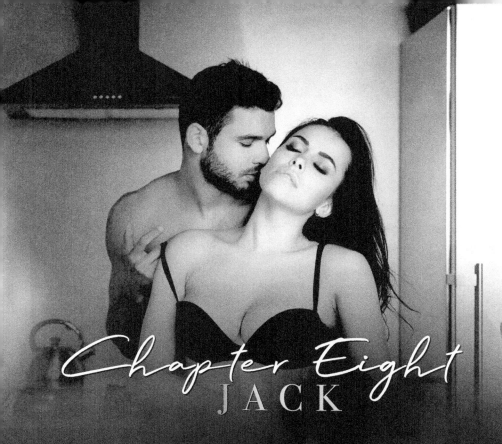

Chapter Eight
JACK

Fuck. I almost lost it. I almost caved in and kissed her.

She wanted it. I could see it in her eyes. In the way her chest heaved in anticipation.

Gah! I dig my fingers into my scalp and tug at the strands of hair, not stopping until I feel the sting.

What the hell is wrong with me? Even if she wanted it, it wouldn't make it right. I know she's underage. I know she's my niece. But it's as if I can't help it. My body is drawn to hers like a magnet.

My hand drops, hovering over the phone in my pocket, my mind warring whether or not to have Matt step in instead of me.

I can't. As soon as I close my eyes, I see Amanda's little face, grief stricken and terrified from her nightmares. It's not just her that needs me, it's Alex, too. The boy needs his father, but if he can't have Austin, I'll do my damn best to step in and fill that void.

There's no doubt that Mexico rocked every one of those kids. Even Pen. She might try to act all put together, but every now and then, I see the frightened little girl.

I've been pacing back and forth in my study while Pen's been in with Dr. Leventhal and it's taken everything in me not to eavesdrop through surveillance.

I need to know if they touched her. So help me god, I'll rip apart heaven and hell if they did. I'm about to pull my goddamn hair out when there's a soft knock at the door.

"Come in." My voice comes out hoarse, strange to my own ears.

It pushes open and Pen's long legs are the first thing I see, followed by the rest of her. I could stare at her all day, but the frowning doctor behind her has me pulling my gaze away. "Dr. Leventhal, is everything okay?"

"Yes. As we discussed earlier, I think it'd be a good idea if I took you up on your offer. I'd like to visit with the kids and Pen every day for at least a week and then move on to weekly visits."

"Of course. I'll have one of the ranch hands take you to your cabin. We've secured one with two bedrooms and a study, but please let me know if you'll need more room."

"That should be more than sufficient." He glances over at Pen, and I can tell he wants to speak privately.

"Pen, would you mind checking in with Mary and asking her to call Sam? Tell her our guests are ready."

She quickly glances at the doctor and then back at me, no doubt realizing what's been said without words. Pen is smart and I wouldn't put it past her to read body language or social cues. Despite her weariness, she gives us a small nod before spinning on her heels and leaving.

It's not until the door has shut that I realize she didn't speak a word the entire time she was in here. "Dr. Leventhal, Pen seems shaken by her session. Is there anything I should be made aware of? Any trauma she'll need extra help with?"

In all honesty, I'm concerned about one type of trauma in particular, but I'm not about to ask it outright.

The doctor grimaces. "Jack, the type of situation they were in... it isn't typical. Even for me, and I deal with extraordinary circumstances. Now, there are things I can't tell you. Things that are said in confidence through our doctor patient relationship." He pauses a little too long for my comfort. I'm about to reach over and strangle the words out of him when he finally opens his mouth to speak. "But I will share this, the fact that she survived her mother's execution and was found clinging to her siblings is something that she'll carry with her for the rest of her life. It's a bond with those two kids that can either help heal her, or be her downfall."

I stagger back, sitting on the edge of my desk. "What are you saying? That she's using the kids like a crutch?"

He brings his fingers to his lips, rubbing at them before responding. "It's too soon to say, but I definitely see the signs of it happening. This is one of the reasons why I'd like daily visits with her and the kids. I'd also like to see how she is with them. That should help me make a better assessment."

"Okay, that won't be a problem. You can come to dinner tomorrow night once you and your associate have settled in."

He nods, his lips pressed into a firm line. "The children adore her. That much is clear. It seems she's taken on a protective role with them and shielded them from most of what transpired, but even so, they'll have to work through their recovery on their own. With emotional support, of course, but on their own."

I nod, even though I'm not sure I entirely agree with what he's saying. I'll have to talk to the other doctor and see what she thinks. They're kids, for Christ's sake. It's not like Pen is coddling them by giving them love and comfort.

I've seen the way she is with them. She has nothing but their best interest at heart. I'm about to tell him as much when there's a knock at the door. "Come in," I call out, hoping it's the ranch hand.

Sure enough, Sam steps through the door with his pearl snap shirt and Stetson. "Sir. You called?"

"Yes, Sam. Dr. Leventhal and Dr. Bower are ready. Please take them to their cabin. I believe their luggage is out by their car." I look over to Leventhal, who's nodding in agreement. "Alright then, Sam here will show you how to work our phone systems. If you need anything at all, call Mary. She'll get you set up."

"Thank you. We appreciate the hospitality." He smiles before turning to walk behind Sam, leaving me to my own thoughts.

I have no clue how this is all going to play out. All I know is that I need a second opinion if he thinks he's keeping Pen away from those kids. She's the closest thing they have to a momma bear, and she's apparently chosen to play the part well.

He said she needs the space to heal, but in my opinion, I think tearing them away will be the last straw that breaks her.

Penelope

That doctor has lost his damn mind. There's no way I'm using the kids as a crutch.

Yes, I knew listening in on his conversation doesn't help prove my maturity to Jack, but I had to know what the looney doctor was going to say. I could feel his gaze on me the entire time we *talked*. Judging. Assessing.

I hated it.

Yes, I have trauma. What person wouldn't after what we went through. But to go so far as to say I'm using the kids so I don't cope? That's just plain wrong.

I made a promise to our mother. A promise I intend to keep.

"Miss Penelope, can I get you something to drink?" Mary's voice calls me into the kitchen. She'd been minding the kids during my time with Leventhal.

"Sorry. Didn't mean to pace out in the hall. I just didn't want to bring all of my baggage in here."

"What's baggage?" Amanda's small voice melts away the tension in my body, letting me smile again.

Of course, Alex doesn't miss the opportunity to sass. "It's all of her crazy."

"I swear." I shake my head as I walk toward Mary, holding

out a glass of her famous lemonade. "Some days I wonder how you're only nine."

"Dad always said I was an old soul." He sniffs, looking at the wall, unable to meet my gaze.

Despite how much of a front he puts on, I know he's affected by our tragedy. Blowing out a breath, I walk over to him and squeeze his shoulder with my free hand. "What'd you think of Dr. Leventhal? You don't have to tell me if you don't want to, but I'd like to know."

"He smells spicy," Amanda adds without prompting, the accurate observation making me chuckle.

"Who smells spicy?" A deep voice cuts into the room, sending a shiver through me. Jack walks in wearing an unbuttoned flannel over a tight-as-sin t-shirt and I have to look away.

Focus. You will not fall for this man's charm and good looks.

Placing my lemonade on the table, I crouch down next to Alex. "We were talking about Leventhal." I answer without looking back, instead I focus my eyes on Alex, who's been staring at the wall. Lowering my voice to a whisper, I try to be reassuring. "Hey, buddy. It's okay to feel what you're feeling. Whatever it is, it's normal because it's you. And you don't have to talk about it until you're ready, okay?"

My words seem to pull him from his thoughts and he finally turns his head, giving me a soft smile and a nod.

Okay, good. At least he's not being swallowed by that darkness in his eyes anymore. I get up from my crouch and turn around, only to come face to face with a towering Jack who's just glaring at me. *Okay.*

He calls to Mary without diverting his eyes from mine. "Mary, would you mind packing up a lunch for the children and me? I'd like to take them on a tour of the property and finish with a picnic by the creek."

Jack and I are still in a staring match as the kids squeal and Mary confirms his request. Finally, unable to take the intensity of his stare, I break away and walk toward the counter. I have nothing to do, so I'm just standing there, with my back to his overpowering figure.

I'm about to leave the room when I feel his warmth behind me.

Jack's chest presses against my back as his lips come down, brushing against my ear. "You're going to tell me why you're smelling Dr. Leventhal, *Princess*. And if it's the wrong answer, he'll be on the first flight out of here."

Goosebumps rise across my flesh. His tone is demanding and laced with an emotion resembling jealousy.

Could this be my answer? The meddling doctor who views my care of the kids like a coping mechanism could be gone in a flash if I play it right with Jack.

I move to glance back at the kids, but the action causes Jack's lips to press against the tender underside of my ear. Sucking in a sharp breath, I try to act unaffected by his touch, but I know it's too late. I feel it in the curve of his lips tilting up in a smile. *Damn him.* Damn him for knowing he wields some sort of power, and damn him for using it against me.

Closing my eyes, I regain my focus. The kids. Despite my wanting the doc gone, he's supposed to be the best and there's no doubt they need all the help they can get.

Taking a step to the side, I break out of Jack's embrace, giving us enough space so I can turn around to face him and speak in a hushed voice. "Amanda was the one to make the observation. I was only agreeing, seeing as his cologne isn't something you could ignore." It's true. The man might be charming, but his signature scent is a little overpowering. At least for my taste.

Jack clenches his jaw, the action making his cheek twitch. He stares at me as if assessing the veracity of my words. Ironic because they are the truth, and if I was being selfish, I would've straight up lied to get the doc out of here.

"Okay." With a curt nod, he looks to the kids and then back at me. "Mary, we'll be leaving in thirty."

And without so much as a glance back, this hulk of a man walks right out of the kitchen and off to god knows where. I'm still staring at the kitchen entryway when Mary comes up next to me, placing her hand on my forearm. "Give him time, sweetheart. He's not used to having family stay with him."

Family. That's what he is. No matter how much I say he's not, he is.

I give myself a mental shake. Whatever the hell my body was feeling right now needs to go straight to hell. If it doesn't, that's exactly where I'll be going because on no planet is what I was thinking okay.

FILTHY CROWN

Chapter Nine

JACK

I squeeze my eyes so tight I see sparks of white. *What the fuck is wrong with me?* I just can't help myself, can I?

Letting out a deep sigh, I rub a rough palm across my face. I need to get my shit together. There's no way Austin would approve of the way I'm handling his daughter. She might not have been his blood, but I knew he loved her just the same. And that man would have my hide if he saw me pressed up against her tight little body.

I groan, sending up a prayer she hadn't felt how her body affected mine. That was *definitely* inappropriate.

Needing to change my train of thought, STAT, I dial one of the sat phones. The roads are tricky up to Hunter's cabin, and I'd be lying if I said I wasn't on edge. There seems to be a dark cloud following our family around and I wouldn't put it past fate to fuck with us once more.

The line rings and rings, but there's no answer. *Dammit.* I'll try again later, knowing the unease in my stomach won't go away until I know they've arrived safely.

Heading upstairs, I take the steps two at a time. It's been a while since I took the time to enjoy my property and I'm actually looking forward to sharing this time with the kids.

I've just made it to the landing when a voice pulls my eyes to the left hallway.

"Jack! I'm so glad I found you." Georgina speed walks toward me as if I were to run away.

I smile while shaking my head. "I've been home this whole time, Georgina."

"Right, but you were locked up in your study for so long." She bats her lashes at me as she takes a couple of steps forward, bringing her body a mere inch from mine. "I just wanted to make sure you still wanted my help with the kids. It doesn't seem Pen likes me very much and I don't want to overstep." With her last word, she brings up a hand, her palm splaying over my chest.

"Yes, I'd like you to help with the kids when it's necessary. I can't be expected to keep an eye on them at all times and run my business at the same time. As for Pen... she's just a teenager. I'm sure it's nothing personal."

Steps on the landing have me freezing, as if I've been caught doing or saying something wrong. In my mind I know that's impossible, but it does nothing to stop the sinking feeling in my stomach.

Turning my head, I see Pen with an unreadable look in her eyes, her hand clutching tightly onto that of her little sister's. "Amanda spilled her lemonade; she needs a change of clothes."

I jerk a nod, moving out of her way and effectively breaking Georgina's touch.

Speaking of Georgina, she pipes up, "Oh, I can take her. It won't be a problem." She smiles at my two nieces, but they both just glare at her, all while Amanda scoots closer to her sister.

Needing to diffuse the tension, I decide to step in. "That won't be necessary. It's clear Amanda is being helped by Pen. If you don't mind, could you please check in on Leventhal and his associate?"

Georgina pouts, but she remains quiet, only giving me a nod before rushing past Pen and Amanda. *Well, that didn't go well.*

Turning back to Pen, I see that she still has the same unreadable look on her face. Not ready to dive into that nugget of emotion, I avoid it altogether. "Be ready in twenty."

I don't even bother looking back. It's been one hell of a day already and it's not even lunch yet. God, I wish it were acceptable to drink whiskey at this hour.

Penelope

Breathe, Pen. Breathe.

I take in a lung full of air before releasing it slowly, needing to calm the fuck down. If Amanda wasn't right next to me, I swear I'd be screaming into a damn pillow.

She's just a teenager.
She's just a teenager.
She's just a teenager.

Getting Amanda quickly changed, I decide to swallow my pride and forget that whole incident. Mom's voice floats into my head, haunting me with her wisdom. *If you want true happiness in coexisting, you must learn to pick your battles.*

The ever romantic actually had a good point with that one. I saw firsthand how she was with Austin, and after years of searching for her Prince Charming, she finally found him.

My heart clenches at the cruelty of it all. How awful is fate to give you your other half only to tear them away?

Even though Jack is in no way, shape or form, my Prince Charming, we still have to co-exist and I still have to convince him to let me take the kids. *So Mom's words of wisdom it is.*

We're back downstairs way before Jack's twenty-minute timeline so I decide to make myself an iced coffee roadie. I snicker, knowing how much it'll bother Jack.

Sure enough, just as I'm pouring the delicious concoction into a travel container, I hear it.

"Again with that nonsense?" Jack shakes his head as his face contorts into one of disgust.

"Hey, don't knock it until you've tried it." I purse my lips to the side and raise a brow, unwilling to give up my lifeblood just because he's bothered by the idea of it.

To my surprise, Jack walks toward me, his face a breath away. I'm unsure of what he's doing until out of my periphery I see him pick up the travel cup, and then right in front of my eyes the man who has been trash-talking the most delicious drink known to mankind takes a sip.

My mouth drops open, still in shock from it all. I never thought he'd *actually* try it. Before I can even ask him how he likes it, he licks his full lips and I swear my lady bits clench at the sight.

"Yeah, that's a no for me." Jack raises a brow while putting the drink down. Meanwhile, I'm still in a stupor.

He finally takes a step back from me and the fog he had me under lifts, the sudden clarity allowing me to reply. "Well, you've always had crap taste, so it doesn't surprise me."

Jack cocks his head back and laughs. "Excuse me? What do you know of my taste?"

Unable to hold back, I let him have it. "Oh, I remember the woman you brought over to my twelfth birthday party." I raise both brows and give him side eye. "That woman was a hot mess in her too-tiny dress for a young girl's party."

Jack's face turns a funny shade of pink. *So he remembers.* "God. That was ages ago. In all fairness, I didn't tell her we were going to my niece's birthday party."

His niece. That would be me. So what in the hell am I doing? Is this flirting?

Mary cuts into my thoughts. "Sir, I've called Sam to pick up your lunch. He'll take it to the creek for you."

"Great. Thank you." Jack doesn't waiver his eyes from mine. "You ready, Princess?" He waits for my nod before turning to the kids. "We're heading to the stables first."

"Horsies!" Amanda squeals. "Are we going to ride?"

Jack's face breaks into a huge grin. "Yes. We'll be riding doubles."

"Doubles?" Alex's blond brows push together.

"That's when two people ride on one horse," I add, trying to remember the last time I saddled up.

"Exactly. Still remember how to ride, Pen?" Jack asks.

I smile and nod. "Yes, it's like riding a bike. Well, not literally, but the muscle memory of it all. Once you learn it you can't unlearn it. That's what the old colloquial saying means, anyway. Not that riding a bike is anything like riding a horse." I stifle a groan, realizing I'm rambling. Rambling because I'm nervous. Why am I nervous?

Probably because my subconscious knows that I'll be in close proximity to this beast of a man all afternoon. Equal parts thrilling and terrifying. Thrilling because it will give me the opportunity to prove myself, but terrifying because every time I'm around him, I fall into my old thoughts of adoration. Only this time, they're mixed with lust. *Not a good thing.*

Thankfully, Jack is either oblivious to my inner freakout or is just being nice and chooses to ignore it. "Alright then, shall we?" He extends a hand toward the back door.

Clearly not holding any of my reservation, both kids line up in front of him, ready to take on the day. Good. They need to have fun after the heavy morning we've all had.

Suddenly, the sound of horseback riding and a picnic doesn't sound too bad.

FILTHY CROWN

Chapter Ten
PENELOPE

God, his property is gorgeous. The snow-peaked mountains make for the perfect backdrop as we ride along the fields. I have Amanda with me and Jack has Alex. Both kids are thrilled with our new adventure and haven't stopped chattering since we left the stable.

"All of this is yours?" Alex's eyes are wide as he takes in the scenery.

"Sure is. And one day it can be yours too, if you want it." Jack smiles, oblivious to the minefield he just stepped on.

I scrunch my nose and frown. The only way it can belong to Alex is if he gives it to him outright or if he wills it to him after his death. Based on his 'one day' comment, I'm betting he's thinking of the latter.

Apparently not one to miss my facial cues, Jack cuts into my morbid thoughts. "What's wrong, Pen?"

I shake my head, not wanting to answer. It's not exactly the right time to discuss postmortem gifting. If the kids didn't catch his meaning, I sure as heck won't bring it back up.

Jack rolls in his lips, unpleased with my lack of response, but thankfully drops it. "We're riding out to an empty cabin. I want to show you guys what we do for people here."

"And what is it you do, exactly?" I take on a playful tone, trying to ease the tension between us.

Jack takes the olive branch, his lips spreading into a full smile. "I give the gift of escapism."

My brows raise at his statement. "That is quite the gift. What I wouldn't give for some of that."

A funny look crosses his face before he blinks it away. "I'm sure we can figure something out. Riding is a good start, but what did you used to do for fun back home?"

That's a no-brainer, don't even have to think before answering. "Read. Not a day went by where I didn't pick up a book or my phone with the e-reader app."

"Your phone. That reminds me, we're going into town tomorrow to get you your replacement. I'll need you to come with me in order to pick one out so we can make sure it has that e-reader stuff on it."

I nod and pull back a snort. The way he said that makes me think he's not good with technology. But either way, I'm thankful for his offer. I totally would've done it myself, but I'm not eighteen, so I can't open up an account on my own. Not for the phone I wanted, anyway.

It's moments like these that make me realize how limiting

my own age is. I swear, I feel like an old lady inside of a teenager's body and sometimes I forget.

My soul is cynical and weary. If only they awarded contracts based on that. I'd be getting all sorts of senior discounts.

"I see something!" Amanda shouts, pointing toward a thick mass of Aspen trees. I'm surprised she can see anything other than the leaves. We'd been ascending toward the tree-line, my eyes making out a trail the closer we get.

"Yes, that's the path to our cabin. Sam should've delivered all of our stuff by now. He's much quicker with his ATV." Jack takes off ahead of Amanda and me, leading us down a trail so stunning I'll have to remember to come back for hiking.

Before I know it, our horses are trotting toward a substantial A-frame cabin. It's stunning, with massive windows on both the front and back. You can practically see through it to even more green and white trees. "Wow, if it's this pretty on the outside, I can't wait to see what the inside is like."

Jack chuckles. "And that isn't the half of it. There's a creek behind the property. You have to go down another smaller path, but the view is breathtaking. It leads to a little waterfall, making for the perfect picnic spot."

Alex's face lights up at the sound of that. "Can we go in the water?"

"Sorry to be a Debby Downer but I didn't bring us bathing suits." And it's not like we have any with us. Our stuff is still being shipped from California.

Jack winks at me. "I've got you covered. Sam delivered the stuff Mary picked up for you on Friday."

My eyes go wide, but then I shouldn't be surprised. My

closet is fully stocked. "Well, you've thought of everything, haven't you?"

We've dismounted and the kids are running ahead of us, eager to see the inside of our treehouse cabin. I turn to see Jack and he's making a face. "That's what any good guardian would do. We take care of our kids. And that includes telling them things they don't want to hear, like how they need to go to college. You know we still need to talk about that, right?"

I smirk, batting my lashes. "Yes, Daddy." Running a hand along his forearm, I bite my lip for effect and boy, does that make him turn red.

"Penelope," Jack warns.

"What?" I try to act innocent, but I know I've poked the bear. For whatever reason, older me affects this man. I'm not sure if he finally sees me or if this is all just in my head.

Whatever the case, I'm having too much fun to stop my teasing.

Jack reaches the door, the kids bouncing up and down on their toes, eagerly waiting for him to open it.

As soon as it swings out, the kids fly inside. I'm about to follow when there's a sharp tug on my ponytail, making me jerk back.

Falling into Jack's chest, his arms wrap tightly around me. "Be a good little girl, Princess. You don't want to be spanked by Daddy."

All air leaves my lungs, making me gasping for air. *Oh my god. Did he just say that?* I'm stock-still wondering what in the hell just happened when Jack drops his arms and walks away. Not even glancing back to see the puddle he's left me in.

Taking a minute to collect myself, I let what happened sink in.

Jack flirted. *With me.* It's the boldest he's ever been, and I'm not sure how I feel about it. I'm still mad at him and I'm very much still disappointed with how he left me four years ago. All that resentment can't just evaporate in twenty-four hours, can it?

"Hurry up, Pen! You have to see this!" Alex calls from somewhere up above me.

Stepping into the cabin, I see that it's minimally decorated to not detract from the massive windows. What little furniture there is looks to be luxe though, with rich leather and intricate wood carvings.

To my right there's two long couches that run parallel to each other so that you can enjoy the view from either the front or rear windows, and behind that there's a massive stone fireplace.

To my left sits the small kitchen. It might be small, but the appliances are all high-end and the countertops are all in a rich butcher block.

"You like?" Jack asks from a recessed hallway by the kitchen.

I laugh at the ridiculous question. "Who wouldn't?"

"You'd be surprised." He makes a face and is about to say something when a phone ringing cuts him off.

He pulls out a phone with a stubby antenna. "Hello? Hey, Matt." Jack smiles at something his brother says over the line. "Yeah, sure. That sounds good." Another pause has me wondering what they're talking about. "Okay, I'll let her know. Just call me when you're heading this way."

Oh, wow. They must've been talking about me. Sure enough,

Jack fills me in as soon as he presses end on the call. "That was Matt. They're staying up at Hunter's cabin for a bit, but then they're all coming back to our place. He said Hunter wants to see you and the kids. He feels just as bad as we all do and he wanted you to know that he would've been here when y'all first got here if he would've known. He doesn't want you thinking he doesn't care."

My eyes mist up at the thought of Hunter, the most hardcore manly man, getting all emotionally supportive of us. Despite my long-held beliefs, these Crown brothers have made a good case against my argument that all men are worthless.

"I would love that." I'm taking a step toward him when a tiny human yells my name.

"Pen! Are you coming?" Alex calls from above and I look around quizzically, wondering where he is.

"He's up in the loft with Amanda. They hightailed it to their own private lookout. It's actually pretty cool up there. You should check it out." He points to a ladder attached to the wall.

Holy crap. I thought that was decorative. Turns out it takes you up to a secret loft.

Not wasting any time, I head up to see what the fuss is about.

I smile as soon as I see the kids laying on plush beanbags. They're both looking through a massive porthole window into nothing but beautiful nature. Jack was right. I definitely wouldn't want to miss this.

FILTHY CROWN

Chapter Eleven
JACK

I'm going to hell. That's it. That's all there is to it.

My cock grew with every step Pen took up that ladder. I couldn't help it, watching her juicy ass, imagining how those globes would feel in my hand as I slammed into her from behind.

Shit. I squeeze my eyes shut, trying to push those images out. That was an hour ago and I still can't get the flashes of temptation out of my head.

We've finished eating and are about to enjoy the private waterfall when the clothes start coming off. *Lord help me, a man can only take so much.*

Pen removes her tank top and cut-off shorts, revealing a black bikini that leaves little to the imagination. *Jesus.* I really

Sure, I'm enjoying the view now, but I can't help and imagine the college boys that will drool over Pen when she takes this two-piece with her.

The kids squealing and splashing pulls me from my murderous thoughts. They both stay on the edge but Pen, being the adventurous girl she is, heads straight for the fall itself. She's about ten feet in when she lets out a yelp, going under not two seconds after.

Before I can even think, my legs jump into action. I'm sprinting toward her, pulling her into me as soon as I've reached her flailing body.

"Are you okay? What happened?" My hands roam her, trying to see if something bit her.

Instinctively, her legs wrap around my waist as I haul her closer to me, pressing my large hand against her back and causing her chest to rub against mine. I have to swallow a groan as her hard little nipples rub on my bare chest, the small contact sending blood rushing south.

Abort. Abort. Abort. A voice inside is telling me to put her down, but my limbs don't obey.

"My ankle. I rolled it. I guess my foot must've gotten stuck between the rocks." Big doe eyes blink up at me, the action causing beads of water to cascade down her cheeks.

My heart is pounding a mile a minute at the thought of her being hurt, and I wonder if she can feel how much it affects me.

"Fuck," I hiss before pressing my lips to her forehead. "You scared the shit out of me, Pen."

She wraps her arms around my neck, all while biting her bottom lip and releasing a soft whisper that has my cock hardening in a flash. "Sorry, Daddy."

I close my eyes and suck in a sharp breath. "What are you doing, Pen?"

My cock is fully awake now, begging to get out of my thin swim trunks and rub all over her sweet heat. It would take seconds to slide that tiny triangle of fabric to the side and shove myself deep into her cunt.

Just then, my length twitches against her folds, her eyes going wide at the realization.

I'm about to move her so her core isn't directly on my erection, but she shakes her head no, gripping onto me tighter.

My wicked little girl looks over her shoulder, making sure the kids are occupied and completely unaware of what's going on beneath the water. *Christ, this is not good. I should stop this right now.*

"Penelope," I warn for what feels like the millionth time. This is so wrong. She's my niece. She's so damn young. If Austin were alive and saw me holding her like this, he'd fucking murder me.

"What? You're not doing anything wrong. You're just taking care of me. Don't you want to take care of me?" She begins to rub herself on my length, all while I'm frozen like a statue, save for my ticking jaw.

I'm unwilling to be a participant in this sinful act, but damn if I don't enjoy her little whimper when her clit hits the top of my aching cock. She keeps rocking against me as my fingers press deeper into her full hips before trailing down to her ass and squeezing. *God, they feel even better than I'd imagined.*

I need to stop. This shit can't go any further. "Penelope. We can't do this."

She lets out a little moan and I practically come in my trunks. "There's no we. You're not doing anything wrong, Uncle Jack. It's all me."

I close my eyes and take in a deep breath. Anything to keep me from rutting into her like a wild animal. Just then, her hand snakes into my shorts, pulling all of me out. She gives my dick one hard stroke and I swear I see God.

Using the tip of my cock, she slides her bikini to the side, rubbing the fat head up and down her slit.

Fuuuuuck. That feels good. Too good. With a little thrust, I'd be inside. No! I'm fighting myself when she lays my length flat against my stomach before pressing her soft folds against my bare flesh. Pen is grinding herself up and down the shaft and I know I'm about to make a mess.

"Penelope. No," I grit out, low enough for just her and me to hear. A quick glance toward the kids shows me they're still busy collecting stones along the shoreline.

"Just a little more," she whines, pressing herself harder against me with slow deliberate grinds pulling the sweetest sounds from her lips. "Almost there, Daddy."

An animalistic rumble comes from somewhere deep inside me. I'm a weak man. Her words slay me. *She wants me. She needs me. Her daddy.*

In that moment I know. I want to be the only man to make her feel good. The only man to ever make her whole.

Even with this realization, I know I'm not supposed to touch her. "I can't touch you, Princess. You know it's not right."

Pen presses her body flushed with mine, her lips brushing

against my neck before her words wreck me once more. "It's okay, Daddy. Don't move. Let your little girl take what she needs."

Jesus christ. I know I must be leaking because, holy fuck. What can I say to that?

Before I can say anything in response, Pen rubs her slick folds up and down my length, my jaw clenching so tightly my teeth are about to crack.

Despite how fucking good this feels, I don't dare move; I don't dare breathe. My hands remain on her hips, unwilling to move back to her ass for fear of angling her just right.

I can't do that. I can't slide inside her. It's wrong. *This* is wrong.

Her words keep echoing in my head. *'Don't move.'*

My mind might not agree with this, but my body has taken her order as gospel.

I'm doing the best I can to comply, but I know I can't hold out much longer. That's a line I won't allow myself to cross, even if I have to leave her in the water with an injured ankle.

Better that than fuck her right here and now.

I'm warring with myself when she begins to shake in my arms, shuddering against me while her whimpers come out choked. Her climax hits her not twenty feet away from her oblivious brother and sister, and in that moment, I couldn't be more thankful for the murky water.

As she's biting down on my shoulder, coming down from her high, a wave of rage hits me. *I'm one sick fuck.* Despite knowing this was wrong, I enjoyed every bit of it. Hell, given a few more seconds, I know I probably would've thrown all morality out the window and fucked her raw.

This is all so damn sick. I'm her damn guardian. I'm supposed to be protecting her, not corrupting her.

Pen is limp in my arms, her climax having ebbed. Needing to right this situation, I carry her bridal style while tucking myself back in and making sure her bottoms are in place. *I need to get us out of the water.*

As soon as we've reached the shoreline, I place her on a smooth rock and head inside, not even looking back, rage and shame filling every cell of my body.

I need to get away from her and take care of this raging hard-on before I do something that will make me hate myself more. What I'm about to do now is bad enough. There's no doubt she'll be front and center in my mind as I splatter all over the shower walls.

Like I said before, I'm going to hell. That's it. That's all there is to it.

FILTHY CROWN

Chapter Twelve
PENELOPE

It's been two weeks since the creek and Jack hasn't looked me in the eye since. We were supposed to go get my phone, but he's been radio silent, giving me the bare minimum in communication.

I mean, can I really blame him? I was like a horny possessed stage five clinger. Hadn't even been around him for twenty-four hours and I was throwing myself at him like my life depended on it.

Groaning into my hands, I try to shove the memory of his massive length out of my mind but it's useless. I'm like an addict wanting more and the knowledge that he's no good for me does absolutely nothing to assuage the need.

He's way older, my uncle—though the lines on that are grey—and he's already abandoned me once before. Who's to say he won't do it again? Besides, I've already made up my mind that I'm leaving with the kids when I turn eighteen.

God forbid he goes and abandons them too after they grow attached. Nope. I won't let that happen. Over my dead body.

"Pen, are you coming downstairs?" Amanda calls me from my bedroom door.

"Yes, pumpkin. Are the guests here?"

My little sister nods enthusiastically. "Yes, and Ashley is here too."

The men of WRATH are here with their families. Jack wanted to thank them for what they did for us and they'll be staying for a couple of days through the weekend. To say that I'm excited is an understatement.

I've never been one for girlfriends, but everything that I've been through recently has me jonesing for some girl time. Ashley offered when I last saw her and I'm definitely taking her up on that now. "Okay, I'll be right down. Let me get dressed first."

Amanda scurries off while I happily drag myself out of bed. Maybe I can get Mary to whip up some of her delicious cinnamon rolls to take over. Those things are gold.

I'm putting on the finishing touch of gloss on my lips when a shadow by the door catches my eye. Turning, I see Georgina standing there with a skintight top and skinny jeans.

"Can I help you with something?" I look at her with apprehension. Yes, she's technically the live-in housekeeper, but she knows my room is off limits. I made that clear on day one.

"I just wanted to see if you needed new linens." She gives

me a smile, but I can see it's as fake as her cheery disposition.

"I know where the linen closet is, and I can change them myself. Same goes for the kids' rooms."

She gives me a curt nod and mumbles something under her breath.

"What was that, Georgina?" I am not having any of her disrespect. I don't care what position she holds in Jack's life.

Damn, is he sleeping with her too? Ugh, he's not sleeping with me. He isn't mine, and I need to stop acting like it or I'm setting myself up for failure.

"Nothing, Penelope. I just think that if we're going to live together until you're off to college, we should probably get along. How about joining me tonight for some popcorn and a movie? Maybe a little girl bonding will help us get to know each other a little better and this," she waves a hand between us, "*tension* can go away."

I position myself right in front of her face and speak deliberately slow, "See, under any other circumstance, I would accept. But for some reason, you've disliked me from day one, and whatever you're concocting now feels like a trap. One I will not fall for, so that'd be a hard pass for me." I walk around her and leave her while she opens and closes her mouth like a flailing fish.

Call me cruel, but I've seen her eyes and feel the vibe she's putting out. If I've learned anything in my short life, it's to always trust your gut, and my gut is telling me she's rotten to the core.

Me and the kids are getting out of our four-seater side-by-side when we're ambushed by twins. They look to be about eight and look a lot like Aiden, one of the men on our rescue mission.

A gorgeous dark-haired woman with slate gray eyes comes running behind them, a baby boy on her hip. "Boys, give our guests some space. Forgive them, they're on hyper-drive since being let loose on all this open space." She extends a hand, her eyes friendly and warm. "I'm Bella. Their sister and occasional babysitter. And this here is Ethan, he's my baby boy."

"Wow, you have your hands full with all these boys." I smile, shaking her hand. "We came by to drop these cinnamon rolls off as a thank you for everything the guys did for us."

"Oh, you didn't have to. That's their job. Besides, setting us up with this much needed retreat is thank you enough."

"It's amazing isn't it? I still can't get over all the beautiful trees. Behind this cabin there's also a creek that leads to a small waterfall." My whole body heats at the memory of what happened there.

She smirks, "Sounds like quite the waterfall."

I choke on a laugh. "It is." Looking around, I see people moving about inside the cabin. "Is Ashley here? I wanted to have a chat if that's okay."

Bella points at the twins and Alex playing in an actual treehouse I'd missed the last time we were here. To their left, I see Amanda playing with a little blond girl who has what looks like a parade of dolls going on. "It looks like the kids are all fast friends now. Let me introduce you to the ladies of WRATH."

That's when I see the women close to where the toy parade is. They're all stunningly beautiful. I suddenly feel frumpy in my cutoff shorts and black tank top.

"Pen!" Ashley shrieks, standing up and speed walking toward me. As soon as she reaches me, she pulls me into an embrace as if we were long-lost sisters.

"Ashley, it's so good to see you." I hug her back as best I can without dropping the baked goods in my hands.

"You too, sweetheart." She pulls back and sees the plate I'm holding. "And what's in here? It smells amazing."

"Mary's cinnamon rolls. I brought them over as a thank you."

She tugs at my arm, pulling the plate and handing it over to a redhead who's peeling back the foil before I've even sat down.

We're all in a semicircle with a clear view of the kids playing. It's the perfect spot, with green leaves and white tree trunks as the backdrop. "Let me introduce you to the ladies. You've already met Bella, she's William's wife."

My brows raise because I'm pretty sure she's close to me in age and William has got to be around my uncle's age. If Ashley notices my facial expression, she doesn't say, continuing on with her introductions.

Next, she points at the redhead, who's already got a mouthful of cinnamon roll. "That's Alyssa, she's Hudson's wife and they're expecting their first baby."

Then she points to a blond who's trying to pry the plate of rolls from Bella. "That would be Cassie. She's our stylist and Ren's other half. As you can see, both her and Alyssa are expecting, and they are ferocious over anything sweet."

I chuckle, "Next time I'll be sure to bring extra."

"Yes, please!" They both chime in unison and we all laugh.

"And that's it. Well, Charlotte is inside with Aiden." She rolls her eyes. "They're probably getting it on in some secluded corner of the house. I swear, those two can't get enough of each other."

Bella holds her hand up. "Please stop. That's my dad you're talking about and I don't want to hurl up this delicious roll!"

These ladies are a trip and I can tell that I like them already. Funny thing is, they all look to be in their early to mid-twenties, and each one of them is paired off to an older man of WRATH securities.

"Is that how you all met? Through WRATH securities? Were you all rescued too?" My brows furrow, trying to figure out how these modelesque women all paired off with these gorgeous hunks.

The blonde, Cassie, cackles. "Something like that. The men all met in high school, with the exception of Aiden. He's my husband's big brother and Bella's dad. They all started WRATH securities later on and we all just fell into the mix."

Bella chimes in, "You already know Aiden is my dad, and Cassie is my best friend. So that's sort of how she met my uncle Ren. Then there's Ashley, who's my husband's little sister and has known the men all her life."

Ashley smirks. "Then there's Charlotte who knew Aiden from when he and her older sister dated."

My brows raise and I feel my forehead get tight. That must've been a doozy. Can't imagine Charlotte's sister took too kindly to that.

"What about you, Alyssa?" I ask, wanting every detail.

The redhead gives me a mischievous smile. "Hudson is my stepbrother. That's how I met the ladies."

Oh my. All sorts of taboo age-gap going on here. Unable to keep my mouth shut, I blurt out, "It's like you're all of my favorite book tropes come to life!"

The ladies let out a collective cackle, and I can't help but join in. "Well, maybe someday someone will write our love stories." Ashley smiles at the lot of us. "Now, before we continue with our conversation, there's something you need to know. We don't do secrets and we never do judgment. If you're okay with that, then, welcome to the ladies of WRATH."

All of the women nod, humming their agreement.

"But I'm not with any of the WRATH men? How could I be a lady of WRATH?" My brows push together, feeling like I've won the friend lottery and having done nothing to earn it.

Ashley waves her hand. "That's semantics. You're an honorary member."

I blush, overcome with emotion. Here I was, putting myself out there for a new friendship with Ashley, and I gained a whole tribe. I'm about to tell them as much when a familiar voice cuts me off, sending a visible shiver running through me.

Turning toward the voice, I see Jack strutting through the pathway. He's talking to Hudson, the man who rescued us from the room of horror.

Just then, the vision of my mother's body lying on the ground flashes through me and I let out a choked sob. I'm overcome with emotion, my body breaking out into a cold sweat as I begin to shake.

I'm squeezing my eyes shut when I feel strong arms engulf me in their warmth. The scent of leather and cigar surrounds me, and I immediately melt into the hard body it belongs to.

It's Jack. I'd know that smell anywhere.

Blinking my eyes open has me staring straight into his. God, I've missed them. He'd denied me this connection for days and I've been a starved woman.

Staring deeper into his hazel eyes, I'm brought back to the present. "Jack. What are you doing here?"

"It doesn't matter. Talk to me, Pen. What happened?" His brows push together, his perfect pout is turning down into a frown.

I blink again, trying to gain my mental footing. "I saw Hudson." Looking back toward the trail, I see he's now much closer standing next to the redhead named Alyssa. "I guess it must've triggered something in me and I saw my... I saw the room back in Mexico."

"God, Pen." Jack snakes his hand behind my head and pulls me forward, his lips finding the top of my head. "You scared the shit out of me."

Tilting my head up at him, I give him a cheeky smirk. "Seems I'm in the habit of doing that."

His face flushes red and I wonder if he's remembering the waterfall like I am.

Jack clears his throat and releases his very tight grip on me, rubbing his hands up and down my arms before finally pulling away completely. "Are you okay now? Do you want me to call Dr. Leventhal? This is definitely something you should discuss with him."

My palms go up in supplication. "Please, no! I'm fine. I promise. And yes, I agree. I'll bring it up with him tomorrow."

He nods, pointing toward the cabin. "Okay. I'll be inside

talking with the men. Holler if you need anything. Maybe I can follow you and the kids back home when you're ready."

The corner of my mouth lifts into a half smile. He's genuinely worried, and it shows. "That sounds good."

With another nod, he disappears with Hudson to discuss god knows what. After what just happened, I don't even want to know. It'd probably trigger another memory. Something I definitely don't want to deal with right now.

I'm staring in the direction they went when a woman clearing her throat has my attention falling back on the ladies of WRATH.

The blond one named Cassie purses her lips and raises a brow. "So aside from the freak out, that was interesting."

My face flushes with heat and I'm sure I resemble the bottom of her Louboutin flats. Ashley wasn't kidding when she said she was their stylist. Girl has great taste.

Bella shoves at her shoulder. "Give the girl a chance. She just met all of us. You can't start prying secrets from her."

Cassie snorts. "How else are we supposed to break her in?"

Ashley places her hand on my shoulder. "Seriously, don't let her bully you into anything."

"I'm no bully!" Cassie scoffs in indignation.

I shake my head and laugh. "I'm more concerned that you guys think whatever that was between Jack and me was more interesting than a full-blown panic attack. I swear it felt like I was going to die."

Alyssa flashes me a sympathetic smile. "We've all been in shitty situations and understand they're a part of trauma. Remember, no judgment. Ever."

"Well, as much as I appreciate your friendship, there's nothing going on there. Jack is my uncle, and that's that." I try to be convincing with my words, but I don't think anyone's buying it.

Ashley's the first to call me on it. "Last I recall, you said something along the lines of 'he's not my uncle.'" With a raised brow and pursed lip, she begs me to argue.

"Fine, there's something there. But it's totally one sided and shouldn't even be a thing. I don't trust him, and even if I did, he doesn't feel the same about me."

Bella's face contorts into one of incredulity. "Girl, the way he was holding on to you like you were the most precious thing since sliced bread says otherwise. That man looks like he worships the ground you walk on. Just you wait."

Ashley nods vehemently. "I agree. Give it some time. Whatever it is will work itself out between you two."

I snort. "Yeah, when pigs fly."

The girls finally drop the topic of Jack and me, moving on to their plan for the next couple of days, making me promise I'll come back for another visit. I quickly promise I will and drive conversation as far away from my non-love life as possible.

FILTHY CROWN

Chapter Thirteen
JACK

"**W**hat do you mean you don't know?" My teeth are about to turn to dust, I'm grinding them so hard.

"We mean, we don't fucking know." Hudson growls, refusing to drop my gaze. This is what I get for being in a room full of alphas. "It's not typical cartel behavior, that's for damn sure. We've been digging, asking our sources for info, but everyone either doesn't know or this is something only high-level members had access to."

"I don't understand. Don't get me wrong, I'm thankful as hell they didn't sexually abuse her. I just want to know the *why*."

"So far, all we have is that the guards were ordered not to touch her. Her mom was free game but not her." Hudson drops that bomb and my stomach sinks. I wonder how much Blanca suffered at the hands of these monsters.

William thankfully cuts into my thoughts, though the image he paints isn't much better. "If Pen's a virgin, they could've wanted her for the market."

Hearing this makes my blood boil. Is my little princess a virgin? She sure as hell didn't act like it under the waterfall. No, she climbed me like a wanton woman.

My cock twitches at the memory. *Fuck.* Now is not the time.

Hudson looks sheepish as he asks, "Is she? A virgin?"

My body heats to the point of discomfort. Looking out the massive picturesque window at the women sitting outside, I grit out my answer. "I have no fucking clue."

"Tiiiimberrrr," Titus bellows into the room.

My brows push together, wondering what in the world he's talking about. Meanwhile, Hudson coughs, trying to hide a chuckle.

"What?" I bark, not in the mood to be out of the loop.

Hudson answers, "It's nothing. Titus has this thing where when one of us men falls for their girl, he says they fall like a log, hence he yells timber." I glare at him and he quickly holds up his hands. "Hey, I'm just the messenger."

Turning toward Titus, he has this annoying smirk on his face. "I just call it like I see it, brother. All the women out there are taken, save for Pen and your five-year-old niece, and I know you weren't looking at *her* that way."

I run a hand over my face, letting out a slow breath. "I don't know what you're talking about."

I'm a fucking liar. I very much know what he's talking about.

"Look, I'm going to lay it out there. Each and every woman

out there came with an insane story and it was a battle to get to our happily ever after. But man, was it worth it. I'd slay a million dragons if it meant I could hold my woman in my arms. And *that* is how you were looking at Pen."

"Even if that were the case, if I truly felt that way, I couldn't do anything about it. She's seventeen and my niece for fuck's sake." My skin grows tight, unable to contain all of my emotions.

"Legally, she's not your niece anymore. And as for her age? Just wait a couple of months and that won't be an issue." William speaks this matter-of-factly, and I wish I could be as certain as he is about how to move forward with these feelings, but I can't.

"Her turning eighteen doesn't change the fact that she's so young, she's just a girl. Or the fact that my brother would murder me if he were still alive." The reasons why this would be so wrong keep looping in my head.

"Excuse me if I'm overstepping," Titus lifts a brow, waiting for my nod to continue. Once he gets it, he drops a truth I can't ignore. "Pen, just like our women, has been through hell and back. Based on her background info, it doesn't seem like she had an easy childhood either. At least not before her mom met your brother. Point being, she's not the little girl you thought you once knew."

William cuts Titus off. "And as for your brother murdering you, all you have to do is ask yourself if your feelings are serious. As in, do you want her to be your forever? If so, I think Austin would've eventually come around. Hell, I did when Titus went after my sister."

Titus snorts, "It took you a minute, though. At least it wasn't like Aiden when *you* went after *his* daughter. It took him about a year."

I chuckle. "You men have quite the story. Who thought your security service would come with relationship advice."

"Hey, this isn't typical for us." William quarks his lips into a half smile. "But finding a brother with a similar love life hangup, we couldn't *not* say anything."

"Whatever the reason, I appreciate it. For everything." I glance back at Pen and can't even imagine a world where she wasn't in it. That's what would've happened had these men not retrieved her from Mexico.

"And we aren't done. So far, there's no word that they're looking for Austin's kids. But based on experience, they don't like to leave loose ends, and leaving living relatives like children is typically considered a loose end to them." Hudson looks at me apologetically. "The one thing making this different is how they treated Pen and the kids. Alex and Amanda weren't subjected to the brutal discipline of the cartel and only suffered starvation and sub par living conditions."

I snort sardonically, "*Only*. As if that weren't bad enough."

"Hey, I'm only saying that isn't typical behavior." Hudson tries to smooth over my ruffled feathers.

"Neither is the fact that they didn't sexually abuse Pen. That's highly atypical," Titus adds, making a violent shudder run through me. Those words shouldn't even be in the same sentence as Pen's name.

"If you must know, I'll ask her. I don't want anyone else talking to her about it and risking a panic attack like she had outside." My eyes flit to her, finding she's immersed in conversation. She looks happy. The realization making my chest fill with warmth.

"Of course. In the meantime, we'll keep digging and let you know if we catch wind of the cartel coming for the kids. We do suggest you pad your security until we've figured everything out. Maybe have a couple of men stationed outside your main house and a couple more throughout the property."

"No," I forcefully rush out. "We've alerted all the ranch hands to our current situation. They know to be on the lookout for any unauthorized *guests*."

The men look at each other but remain quiet, so I continue, unwilling to give an inch on this. "The kids need stability right now. Seeing bodyguards will only alert them to the fact that they aren't safe and that will definitely hamper any of their progress. The ranch is closed off from the outside and we have more than capable staff here who know what to do in case we have unwanted intruders. Let's not add more security until absolutely necessary. Just keep me informed, and as soon as you have confirmation that the cartel is looking, then that's when we'll implement the additional guards."

They all nod in agreement. I can sense their hesitation, but I'm only doing what I think is best for the kids.

With Amanda still having nightmares and Pen having panic attacks, I'd like Leventhal to work his magic a little longer before I introduce the fact that they still could be in danger. Damn, nobody said parenting would be easy, but having to make decisions like this is downright inhumane.

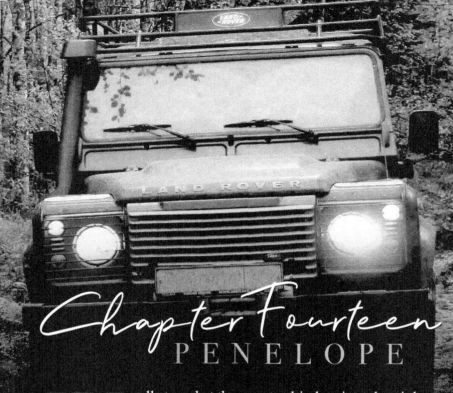

Chapter Fourteen
PENELOPE

We all stayed at the guest cabin late into the night— *way past the kids' bedtime*—but we were all having so much fun.

The kids got along great, and I absolutely adore the ladies of WRATH. I hope they keep coming back to vacation here. It'd be nice to have the female company.

Wait a minute. I yawn into my coffee, peering up at Amanda and Alex who are busy squabbling over who gets to eat the last piece of bacon. The kids bickering and my lack of sleep must have my head messed up because I know I don't have plans of staying here past the summer.

"Stop fighting, guys. I can make you some more bacon if you're still hungry. But you have to eat all of your eggs first." I

They grumble, but they do as they're told. Thank god. I don't have the energy for much more right now.

"Morning." Jack's deep voice has my body coming alive, giving me a quick jolt of energy even caffeine couldn't produce. "Y'all are definitely Crown kids."

"How so?" I smirk, wanting him to look me in the eye once more.

"All of the Crown brothers can put away an entire packet of bacon in one sitting."

The tone of the room takes a somber one as we all remember that one brother is no longer with us. Jack grimaces, noticing what his words have done, but I look him in the eye and shake my head, hoping he understands he did nothing wrong.

We can't walk around eggshells and not talking about our parents would be more tragic than undergoing the sadness whenever they're brought up.

Needing to liven the mood up, I put on the biggest smile I can muster. "You guys want to join the WRATH kids for a playdate today?"

They both beam up at me, nodding with enthusiasm. I'm about to tell them I'll take them up there after breakfast when Jack cuts in. "I can have Mary or Georgina take them, but you're coming with me."

The way he says that sends chills up my spine. "Oh, am I?"

He raises a brow, tone steady and strong. "Yes. We're going into town. It's time you had your own phone."

I give him a small nod, not wanting to show him just how excited I really am. I've been watching the market on Mary's laptop, but it would make it so much easier if I had a phone on me at all times.

I've almost regained all that I lost while we were in Mexico. I just need a little more and it'll be enough to get me and the kids set up once I turn eighteen. Sure, we won't be living anywhere as nice as this, but it'll be safe and it'll be home.

I was so excited about the idea of the phone that the rest of his words are just now catching up to my brain. "Wait, I'll only go if Mary *and* Georgina go together or if only Mary goes. I don't trust Georgina."

Jack's brows raise. "I'm not sure why you don't like her. She's worked here for two years now and I've never had a problem."

It's my turn to raise a brow. "It's not that I don't like her. That's just a byproduct of my not trusting her." I take a sip of my coffee, trying to find the right words to say. Finally, letting out a huff, I give him the only grounds I have. "Look, call it women's intuition. There's something that doesn't sit right with me when it comes to her and I'd sooner trust Sparky the horse than her with my brother and sister."

A snort comes from behind me and I see Mary is refilling the kids' orange juice. She must have snuck in mid conversation. "Don't worry, darling. I'll take the kids."

Looking up at her, I try to convey all of my gratitude with a smile. "Thank you, Mary. That makes me feel a million times better."

"Not a problem at all, dear. Amanda and Alex are a pleasure."

Just then, Alex holds up his plate. "More bacon, please."

I chuckle. "A pleasure and a bottomless pit for bacon, too."

"Thank goodness I've stocked plenty." Mary skirts around

the table and heads toward the fridge where Jack is silently standing.

He's been watching my interaction with Mary, a curious look in his eyes. Finally blinking whatever was going on in his head away, he comes back to life. "Be ready in thirty. And for goodness' sake, put some more damn clothes on."

"Yes, Daddy," I mutter under my breath as the kids giggle and Jack storms out of the kitchen.

He keeps stealing glances at my bare legs like they're going to grow a limb and slap him. I'm wearing a white flowy halter dress and some wedged heels. Same as what I was wearing this morning.

He may not like my little dress, but I do, and I'll be damned if I let a man tell me what to wear. "Why don't you take a picture? It'll last longer."

Jack lets out something between a growl and a snarl. "I thought I told you to put some more clothes on."

"I grabbed a cardigan." I hitch my thumb toward the back, where I chucked it.

"It doesn't count if it's not on your body."

"What's it matter right now, anyway? You're the only one who can see me." My eyes narrow into tiny slits as a devious smile spreads across my lips. "Or is that the problem, Uncle Jack? You can't stand the idea of seeing this much skin on display?" I can't help but reach out and run a finger up his muscular thigh.

I'm trailing higher up his leg when his hand comes down forcefully on my wrist. "No, Pen. This is wrong."

I pull back my hand like I've been burned, and in a way, I have. His rejection hurts more than the lick of a flame ever could.

"Stop whatever's going on in that gorgeous head of yours, Pen." His large hand lands on my shoulder and squeezes.

Great, I'm getting pity petting. Shrugging him off I try to play it off. "Nothing is going on inside my head, Jack."

I'm pretty sure that didn't sound convincing because he keeps glancing at me, a small smirk playing on his lips. "Yes, that's a big part of the problem."

My brows furrow, trying to piece together what he's saying when it clicks. *He finds me attractive!* I mean, obviously I knew I affected him. I felt exactly how much by the waterfall.

Still, there was a part of me that thought his reaction was more mechanical. One caused by being pressed up against a woman. Any woman.

If what he just said is true, then it was more than that.

"Cat's got your tongue?" Jack's smirk has now morphed into a boyish smile, making my insides go all mushy.

"No. I just wasn't expecting you to be so honest, that's all." I turn toward the window, unable to stare at his profile. It's too beautiful and his words are too much. It was all fun and games when I was tempting a man who wouldn't fully play along.

It was safe. It kept me on target and on task, getting everything ready to leave in a few months. But this? His admission? It tastes too damn sweet, tempting me with the idea of forever. And that's something I'm not willing to do. Not for anyone. Especially someone who's abandoned me before.

"I will always be honest with you, Penelope." His hand finds mine and our fingers intertwine, the connection setting my whole body on fire.

His words give me comfort and fill me with rage all at the same time.

"Tell me then." I glare, unable to hold up years' worth of resentment.

"Tell you what?" He sounds genuinely confused.

"How could you not know? How could you not know that you wrecked me? You left my heart battered and bruised when you walked away and didn't look back. I waited for you every Sunday. Stood by the front window of our home, hoping against all odds that maybe one Sunday would be different. That you'd walk through that door and be my constant again. The one good and solid thing in my life. For five years, you let me need you. You let me love you. And then you vanished without so much as a goodbye." I wipe a rogue tear away, unwilling to shed more for this man. "So now that you know. Tell me. Tell me why you left me."

My whole body is shaking now, vibrating with so much pent-up rage and sadness I feel like I'm coming out of my skin.

"Shit, Pen." His voice is choked with emotion, his hands gripping tightly onto the wheel.

Suddenly the car is swerving onto the shoulder of the road, Jack's jaw clenching so hard I can hear his teeth cracking.

As soon as the car has stopped, Jack turns to me, eyes wild. His mouth parts, but no words escape.

In one swift motion, Jack unbuckles my belt and plucks me

out of my seat, pulling me into his lap.

With my face cupped between his large rugged hands, he lets his lips touch my forehead.

"I'm so sorry, Princess. I'm so fucking sorry." He continues to place reverent kisses all over my face. Forehead. Cheeks. Nose. Chin. But never my lips. Never where I need him the most. "I had no damn clue you were in so much pain."

He swipes the hair from my shoulder, replacing it with soft kisses, the action making my whole body shudder. In that moment, pain and sadness are mixed with need. A hungry need for him to make me whole.

"You wrecked me, Jack. You made me believe it was okay to trust you. *A man.*" That last word comes out choked, betraying what I really feel toward the other sex.

His brows knit together as his eyes search mine. "But you had Austin. I don't understand. He was your constant up until the day he... until he couldn't."

I shake my head and look out the window, not wanting him to see how pathetic I truly feel. I can't let him see the desperate and needy little girl that lies inside, underneath all of my jagged layers. "No. Austin belonged to my mom. She was his knight in shining armor. Her Prince Charming. He was nice to me, and I loved him for loving my mom, but he wasn't there for me. Not like you were."

Jack's strong fingers grip my jaw, turning my face toward his. "Baby, I had no idea our routine meant that much to you."

A soft kiss is placed on my nose while I let out a shaky breath. "It did. I didn't have much back then, but I thought I had you. I looked forward to every Sunday. Even when I had to share you with Alex and Amanda." The pad of Jack's thumb wipes at a tear I didn't know had fallen. "For five years, you showed up like clockwork. We would go to the movies, lunch or even a stroll to the park. You were the one who taught me to ride a bike. It was you who taught me that french fries tasted best when dipped in a milkshake."

We both snort a laugh at that. My eyes fall on Jack's lips. A full pout that's stretched into a full grin. "I still do that till this day."

Finally daring my eyes to look between Jack's tumultuous ones, I see that they're glistening. One of my hands travels up to his chest, pressing the palm to his thudding heart. "Me too."

A silence stretches until it becomes too much for me to bear. "So tell me. Why? Why did you leave me?"

He lets out a slow breath, inhaling deeply before answering. "I was battling my own demons, Pen. My parents had just passed, and I was saddled with their estate. Divvying everything up between the brothers and trying to find out why they left us so soon was all too much. Not to mention I had Dad's silent partner hounding me for his share of everything." He runs a hand through his hair, tugging at the ends. "I honestly had no clue that our outings meant that much to you. It was never my intention to abandon you. At first, I'd always placed the travel up to Austin's place on my schedule. I'd meant to visit, but one thing after another came up and I never ended up making it. Eventually, I just stopped placing it on my calendar. Life got away. You got away."

His hands grip on to either side of my head, bringing my forehead down to his lips again as he whispers words of promise. "But never again, Pen. I'll never let you get away."

Finally, letting myself break down in his arms, I let everything go. All the years of sadness and resentment pour out of me like a broken spigot, spilling years' worth of unshed tears onto his cotton clad chest.

In the cab of his truck and in his arms, my tattered heart begins to mend. Choosing to push all logic or reason out of my head, I give in to the emotions running high. Love. I feel it coming off of him in waves and I lap at it like a thirsty little puppy.

But only time will tell if his words are truth, or if they're the last nail on my dark and lonely coffin.

Chapter Fifteen
JACK

I wrecked her. Wow. All this time I'd been lost in my misery and Pen was under the impression that I'd abandoned her.

Well, shit. I guess in a way I had.

My fingers wrap tightly around the steering wheel, the force making my knuckles crack. I should've known my visits meant something to her. Hell, I played a major role in her life for five years.

Not only did I take her out every Sunday so Austin and her mom could have some alone time, but I also went to every recital, birthday party, and soccer game.

And then four years ago, I just stopped, too consumed with my own issues to realize what impact it would have on a young

I open my mouth to apologize, but nothing comes out. What can words do? Nothing. I need to show her I'm never walking out of her life again.

My mind is busy coming up with ways to show Pen I'm here for good when my sat phone rings. Pulling it out, I click it on.

"Hey, you're on speaker. Pen and I are on our way into town." The only ones who have this line are my brothers and the ranch hands. I need to give them a heads-up Pen can hear. God forbid they say something and she has a panic attack while we're driving.

"Jack, it's Matt. We were getting ready to come back to the ranch when we discovered our gas tank was empty."

My eyes narrow and my heart rate picks up. I know for a fact that his truck was topped off before they left our ranch. That should've been enough gas to get them there and then back down to us.

"Okay, can you siphon some from Hunter's truck and get you guys to a gas station?"

Silence stretches before I hear Hunter's voice, "My truck doesn't have gas in it either."

Fuck. I know this isn't a coincidence. Someone emptied their tanks. Question is, why hadn't they slashed their tires instead. It's much quicker than emptying tanks and equally as effective, if not more, at making a point.

"Okay. The men of WRATH are all up at the ranch. Call them and give them a heads up and tell them it's okay to move on with what we'd discussed last night. If what I'm thinking is right, then the ranch hands aren't going to cut it."

"Sounds good. What about the gas?" Matt asks.

"Pen and I will bring some up for you." I cut a glance over to her and see she's nibbling on her bottom lip.

Reaching over, I give her thigh a squeeze. Looking her in the eye, I whisper for just us. "It's going to be okay."

She gives me a nod, her plump bottom lip dislodging from between her teeth.

A snort cuts through the line and Jace's voice booms into the cab. "I know it's going to be okay. It's these two drama queens acting all concerned."

Rolling my eyes, I finally remove my grip on Pen's leg. "We'll be there in a few. Call the men of WRATH and be vigilant."

"Don't worry about us, brother," Matt speaks as the sound of a gun cocking plays out of the speaker. "Hunter's got a fully stocked arsenal."

I grimace, hoping the reference wasn't too much for the girl sitting next to me to hear. Before he can say anything else potentially damaging, I say my goodbyes and cut the line.

"So I guess this means there's a change in plans?" Pen has a hesitant smile on her face and I want to do nothing more than reassure her everything will be fine, but I can't. That would be a lie, and she and I both know it.

"Looks that way, Princess. Your phone will have to wait just a little longer."

"That's okay. I wouldn't mind another trip into the city with you." Pen bats her lashes, and I swear she could get away with murder when she looks at me like that.

"Can't say that I wouldn't mind it either." I give her a sheepish smile as I direct us toward the last gas station we saw.

"Jack?" Pen's playful tone is gone, worry is now marring her pretty face.

"Yes?"

"Someone did this, right? Took their gas?" She's back to biting her lower bottom lip and I want nothing more than to take my thumb and forefinger and pluck it right out.

"I don't know for sure, but it looks that way. Don't worry, though. We'll get them gas, then they're all coming back to the ranch with us. We'll all be safe there."

She nods before turning her head away.

I might've failed her four years ago, but I'm sure as hell not failing her now. I'll do whatever is necessary to keep her and the kids safe.

"Are we almost there?" Pen pulls her cardigan closed, her delicate fingers working on fastening the buttons.

I chuckle. "Bet you wish you would've put some more clothes on, huh?"

Pen glares at me, and if looks could kill, I'd be six feet under. "I didn't know we were going to be coming up to the mountains." She huffs before muttering, "My dress was just fine for going down valley. There's still snow on the ground here, for fuck's sake."

"Language." I know she's right, but I can't help tease. "We'll be there—"

A doe cuts across the road, catching me off-guard and making me swerve in order to avoid it. I jerk the wheel, praying like hell we don't hit any black ice.

Despite my maneuvering, the truck fishtails into a ditch. In this moment, I'm thankful we weren't further up the road where there are no ditches, just a good ol' precipice leading you to certain death.

Looking over at Pen, I see she's got both hands firmly on the grip handle, her eyes open as wide as they can go.

"I see why they call this the 'oh shit' bar." Pen lets out a shaky breath.

I chuckle, thankful that she's still got her humor about her. "Yes. And on the bright side, we didn't hit Bambi."

She rolls her eyes, but the smile on her lips tells me she finds my joke mildly amusing. *I'll take it.*

I go to press the accelerator, but we don't move. Banging on the steering wheel, I let out a string of curse words. God, this would be just my luck, wouldn't it?

"Are we stuck?" Pen's soft voice takes some of the edge off of my anger, thwarting the pity party I was about to throw myself.

"I think so. I'm going to head outside and see how bad it is. Maybe I can put something underneath for traction."

Pushing the door open, I'm hit with that chilly mountain air. There's snow covering the ditch, but underneath there's icy mud. I let out a slow breath before getting to work, pulling something out of the back to use for leverage.

I give up after about forty minutes of trying. There's no way we're getting out of this without help.

Calling Mary, I let her know we might be awhile and thankfully she tells me she doesn't mind watching the kids, which gives me one less thing to worry about. Finally, heading back inside the truck, I let the interior heat warm me up.

"God, you're a damn popsicle." Pen's soft fingers trace over my cheeks.

"Yeah. Well, it seems our four-wheel drive is no match for these Colorado mountains and mud season. There must be over twelve inches of mud out there."

"What are we going to do? The guys don't have gas, so it's not like they can come out to get us." Pen nibbles on that bottom lip and I groan.

After being out in the cold and dealing with our frustrating situation, my patience is wearing thin. I can't handle her temptation on top of that. A man can only take so much.

"We're between national parks. One of my friends is a ranger to the one north of us and I know he patrols the area at least once a day." I shrug and give her a sheepish smile. "I say we wait him out. It's not like we can hike out of here." Raising a brow and looking her over, I silently tell her 'I told you so.'

"I thought we were going down valley!" She throws her head back, letting it thud against the headrest.

"Look, even if you were dressed in a parka, I wouldn't let us hike it to the cabin. It's too late in the day for that and the road gets narrow, with no shoulder to walk on about an hour up. It would be too dangerous and I wouldn't risk your life."

She quirks a brow. "But you'd risk yours?"

"Not if it meant ever leaving you again." I reach up and caress her jawline with the back of my fingers, loving how soft her skin is. Such a contrast to my dry and calloused one.

She sucks in a sharp breath, her eyes wild and glistening.

"Jack."

I shake my head no. This—whatever this is—is all-consuming, coiling up inside and winding us up to the point of combusting. I've never felt anything like this before and I'd bet my ass that neither has Pen.

Even so, this can't happen. *I won't allow it.*

Penelope's bottom lip trembles, and I swear it's as if she's ripped my heart out with her bare hands. Unwilling to let her feel any pain, my thumb brushes forcefully against her bottom lip.

"Don't, Princess. It's not that I don't want you. It's that I can't have you."

She works her jaw, her eyes narrowing. "Says who?"

"Says the law." My face contorts as the memory of my brother comes rearing front and center. "Says the fact that I'm your *uncle.*"

The corner of Pen's mouth lifts into a lazy smile. "Last I checked, there weren't any cops in this car."

I chuckle and shake my head. "You're trouble."

"But the good kind." Her lazy smile has now transformed into a beautiful grin. One that steals my breath away.

"Definitely, the good kind," I grumble under my breath.

Giving us some space, I lean my body back against the door. Hell, maybe it was a bad idea getting back in the car. She'd be less at risk of me mentally mauling her if I'd stayed outside.

"So what now?" Pen blows out a breath, the sharp exhale making strands of hair go flying.

"Now we wait. It's a matter of time before Ericson comes out this way. Good thing we have gas or you'd have frozen your perfect little ass off."

Pen's eyes go wide at my words, the compliment not going unnoticed. "I'm sure you would've found a way to keep me warm even if we didn't."

I squeeze my eyes shut and groan. Visions of me bending Penelope over every which way flood my thoughts, making my pants instantly tighter.

Pen sucks in a breath, probably having caught sight of my bulge. "I meant you would've given me your flannel or, I don't know, built a fire somehow. You know you're super outdoorsy and one with nature and everything."

My princess loves to ramble when she's nervous, and immediately I feel like an ass. My mind flashes back to Mexico and, despite what the reports say, I wonder if the guards there ever assaulted her. "Hey, Pen. Just because my body reacts to you doesn't mean that I'm demanding anything from you. I never want to make you feel uncomfortable or pressured."

Pen snorts so loud her shoulders shake. "God. What on earth would make you say that? I've literally thrown myself on you, shamelessly flirted and made *you* feel uncomfortable, yet you're under some impression that your dick getting hard for me is a *no go?*"

"Well, when you put it like that…" I rub a hand over my face, dreading where this conversation is going. "Look, I need to ask you something. And you might not want to tell me the truth, but I need it. It's important."

Her face transforms from a cheeky woman into that of a scared girl. Knowing this is something that needs to be asked, I push through any hesitation. The fact that they guys had their gas siphoned is concerning, and maybe her answer can shed some light on our situation.

Chapter Sixteen

PENELOPE

Oh no. Whatever he's about to ask isn't good. His face contorts as if in physical pain, making my stomach knot. "Just spit it out. I'm not exactly a delicate flower, despite what you might think."

He raises a brow. "I don't think you're a delicate flower. You're a precious rose. Breathtakingly beautiful, but downright brutal to those who get caught in your thorns."

I chortle. "I think Georgina might agree with the thorn part."

The corner of his mouth tilts up as he gently shakes his head. "There isn't any easy way to do this, so I'm banking on these thorns to push me away if it's too much, okay?"

I give him a small nod, ready to get this question over with.

"I've looked at the reports from your rescue and nowhere on there is it listed that you were sexually abused. I need to know if this is true, or if they…" His jaw clenches, making his cheek tick. "I need to know if they *touched* you."

My mouth goes slack as the rest of my body goes rigid. Visions of Mexico flood in, the four walls of our keeper's cell closing in on my mind.

It isn't until I feel Jack's hands on my face that I snap out of the fog I'm in. "I'm sorry, what was your question?"

"Did they *touch* you, Pen?" His eyes are intense, the pain palpable in his voice.

"They didn't touch me like that." I shake my head, sending up a prayer of thanks for that small miracle. "They starved us and beat Mom and Austin, but they never touched the kids or me."

Jack's hand falls to my own, his grip tightening on my fingers. "There are a couple of reasons why the next question is really important. I hate to even have to ask, but… are you a virgin?"

My eyes go wide and my mouth parts open. I suppose I knew this question was coming, but hearing it from Jack makes my breath hitch and heart rate spike.

Swallowing the lump in my throat, I give him my answer. "Yes."

The one word is all I can muster. It's no secret I have an aversion toward men, and it wasn't until seeing Jack again that this dormant part of me had awakened.

Finally, I found something men are good for. Too bad it typically comes attached to an emotional minefield. I've barely crossed that line with Jack and I already know my heart has started to get tangled up where it's not supposed to.

Jack licks his lips, his eyes twinkling with hidden secrets I want to pry free. *How many women has he been with? Would I be too inexperienced for him?*

"And the men… they were never inappropriate with you?" Jack's voice comes out low, as if the octave helps to shield me from the memory.

I go to shake my head no when I'm thrown back into that dark room, the smell of iron coating the air.

"Come here, pretty girl." My captor's bulky figure slinks over to me in the dead of night.

I try to press myself against the wall, my feet pushing me back as far as I can go. He's at my feet when Mom shouts, "No! Don't touch my baby!"

She tries to drag her beaten body over to me, attempting to use herself as a human shield. But she's too weak after her last beating and every move she makes is accompanied with a full-body flinch.

"Dumb bitch." The man pulls Mom up by her hair, placing the barrel of his gun to her temple.

"You're the dumb bitch." Mom spits in his face, the bold action earning her a punch to the ribs. Still, she gives the man shit, diverting his attention from me. "Her father is going to have your head."

The asshole tenses at her words, his reaction making my brows furrow. Are they afraid of Austin? Is he the reason we're here?

"Then I'll have my fun with you." He rips the remnants of her tattered shirt, leaving her in nothing but her bra and pants. "Your cunt won't be as tight as

your daughters, but I can watch her while I fuck you, imagining it's her I'm inside."

Bile crawls up my throat as my little brother and sister whimper. Unwilling to let him rape our mom in front of us, I push them both behind me and stand up to the thug, not caring that he's still holding his gun.

"Enough. Leave her alone!"

His eyes cut to me and a slow smile creeps up his thin lips. "Oh, does the princess want some of this?"

"Penelope, no!" Mom shrieks as he flings her against a wall.

I shake my head at her, willing her to be quiet. She's been the one to take the heat these past couple of days, letting them abuse her so they'd spare her children. She can't take much more, and I can't just sit by and keep letting it happen.

The man snarls at my mother's protests. "Quiet, woman. I promise she's going to love it."

The smell of his cheap cologne crawls up my nose and a wave of nausea rolls over me. I pitch over to hurl, but nothing comes out.

"Now, now. No need to be scared, little girl." The tips of his boots are visible through my tear-soaked lashes and I know I'm only seconds away from losing my virginity to this monster.

The man jerks my top up, exposing my breasts to the room. I'm praying my little brother and sister aren't watching, that my mom is shielding them from this horror when the door flings open and another one of our captors comes rushing in.

"What the fuck are you doing!?" He yells at the one still gripping on to my shirt. "Get the fuck away from her. You know the orders, pendejo.*"*

"Pinche cabron. I was only having a little fun. Nobody needs to know." He looks at the other guard like he's an idiot.

"You dumb ass. You think you aren't being watched?" The man points to a camera in the corner of the room. "Follow the fucking orders."

"Follow the fucking orders." I whisper into the haze.

"Baby, what are you talking about? Talk to me. I'm right here." I feel lips press to my temple as strong arms hold me tightly against a muscular chest. *Jack.* His scent of leather and tobacco envelops me, giving me the comfort I so desperately need. "What orders, Pen?"

Jack must've pulled me onto his lap when I fell into my panic induced time warp. Slowly, I come to with the help of Jack's firm hand rubbing circles on my back.

Lifting my own hands, I see that they're shaking, my teeth chattering and lips trembling right along with them. No matter what I do, I can't make them stop.

"You're in shock. God, I'm so sorry. I should've waited to ask. Maybe when we were around Dr. Leventhal."

"No." I turn to face him, burrowing my hands under his flannel. The thought of spending another minute with that shrink has me wanting to come out of my skin. "The dinner with him the other night was enough torture to last a month. *At least.* So don't. Just give me a sec."

Burying my face into the crook of his neck, I inhale deeply and let the feel of his strong body center me.

He presses a kiss to the top of my head but remains quiet, all while his hands continue to soothe me with gentle but firm touches.

Once my body has stilled and the panic has subsided, I let myself sit up. "Touching me."

Jack's brows come together. "What?"

"The fucking orders. Apparently, it was part of their orders to not touch me. At least not in that way.

Jack blinks, his face blank before it grows heated. "Pen, I promise I'll do whatever it takes to keep you safe. They will *never* touch you again."

His chest is vibrating against my hand, the anger and conviction in his voice palpable. "I believe you."

I press myself against him, needing to feel his warmth. Instantly, his powerful arms wrap around me tight and squeeze. "Your pain. I wish I could take it all away. I felt so damn helpless when you went into your head just now. It's like you were stuck in this nightmare and I couldn't reach you. I couldn't pull you out."

I sit back up and cup his handsome face between my palms. "But you did pull me out. You came for me. You saved me when I was in Mexico, and you saved me just now."

His brows drop, matching the downturn of his lips. "How did I save you right now?"

"You're my anchor, Jack. You tether me to reality when I'm drifting away in a sea of desolation." I brush a thumb across his bottom lip, and butterflies swarm in my stomach when he sucks in a sharp breath.

"Pen." He closes his eyes, inhaling deeply.

"Shhh." I press my index finger to his lips before lowering my own onto his.

Jack's body tenses with my kiss, his breathing turning shallow. But he doesn't move. Doesn't kiss me back. The rejection stings, but I try not to let it show. Pulling away, I brave a weak smile. "Thank you. For everything. And even though I'm not fully over what happened four years ago, my heart can slowly heal now. I was a foolish girl and had no clue you were going through your own emotional battles."

After enjoying his embrace for far too long, I finally try to pry myself from his arms.

"Stay, Pen." Jack's fingers dig into my hips, keeping me in place on his lap. "Just a little while longer."

My eyes search his, trying to figure out what he needs from me, but frankly, not caring. Whatever this man needs, I'll give to him freely.

I'm lowering my head back onto his chest when he begins to talk. "You're my anchor too. You and the kids give me purpose. A second chance at redemption after having failed my brothers." He presses another kiss to my forehead while his left hand strokes my hair. "When our parents passed, I wasn't there for them. I should've been the glue that held our family together. Instead, I retreated into the dark pits of my sorrow and left everyone to fend for themselves. Maybe if I hadn't been so selfish, Austin and your mom would still be here. I would've kept him from Mexico somehow. I could've saved him." His words choke out at the end and in that moment, all I want to do is take away his pain.

Sitting back, I run my fingers through his scalp before letting them fall to the back of his neck. "They weren't your responsibility, Jack. No matter how much you want to think they are. Yes, you're the older brother, but that didn't make them your children. Austin was a grown man and you can't keep blaming yourself for his decisions."

Jack's body tenses. "You knew what Austin was doing in Mexico?"

"I didn't. Not the specifics, anyway, and not until we were in Mexico. That's when Mom said something that made me realize it." I shudder at the memory, but Jack is quick to pull me back into the safety of his chest.

"Rest, baby. We don't have to talk about this right now."

Taking his words as the excuse I need to let myself be, I sink back into his chest and focus my attention on the rise and fall of his breath, letting it lull me into the peaceful blankness of sleep.

FILTHY CROWN

Chapter Seventeen
JACK

She's so fucking beautiful, I can't keep myself from pressing a soft kiss to her forehead.

I know it's wrong, but in this moment I can't seem to find any fucks to give. It's been hours since she fell asleep in my arms and every minute has been goddamn torture. Every now and again she wiggles her ass on my lap, her heat rubbing against my aching erection, begging to break free and slide inside her.

Groaning, I let my head fall back, fixing my eyes to the sunroof and begin to count the stars in an effort to kill my raging hard-on. It's dark now and with us being higher up the mountain, the moon and stars shine bright enough to illuminate the interior of the cabin.

I'm on number thirty when Pen's breathing changes and I

know she's awake. "What time is—"

Her sharp intake of air lets me know she can feel what I'm sporting. Of course she can fucking feel me. I'm as hard as a damn rock. My dick is hard every time I'm around her, and all he's got to show for it is my palm.

I'm about to deny his ass once more and lift Pen off of me when she grabs my hands and directs them behind my head, having me hold on to my head rest. "Pen?"

"Shhh." She presses a soft kiss to my lips, her wet tongue taking a tentative swipe of my lower lip. *It's my undoing.*

My hands leave their spot to cup her face, my fingers reaching toward the back of her head and pressing her mouth deeper into mine.

I take like a man starving, being given his final meal. Because that's what this is. Final. Even as I suck on her tongue and swallow her whimpers, I know I can't let myself do this again. *It's dirty. It's wrong.*

Her little ass grinds against my cock, the action driving up the frenzy of our kiss. Her hands are wild, pulling at my hair, roaming my chest and grabbing onto my neck before she lifts herself and straddles me. *Fuuuuck.* Her cunt is pressed right up against me, and so help me god, I can't stop myself from giving her one hard thrust.

She lets out a yelp that turns into a mewl as she grinds herself on top of me; the sound making precum leak. *Christ, I need inside.*

A voice in the back of my head is telling me I need to stop. This needs to stop. But my mouth doesn't get the memo.

Pen whimpers as I break our kiss, my lips trailing down her

jawline and onto her neck. Dipping to the hollow, I suck in the tender flesh and taste her. *Mine.* Something inside me snarls, threatening to kill anyone or anything that dares come near.

Here, in the confines of my truck, she's mine. Nobody to bear witness to this debauchery. Nobody to see this old man grinding his cock on a young virginal pussy. *Young.* The one word echoes in my head, and realization of what I'm doing slowly trickles in.

Fuck. She's young. *Too* young. I know the age of consent is seventeen here, but even then, I'm too old and surpass the Romeo and Juliet law. If I touched her and anyone found out, my ass would go straight to jail, and then who'd take care of the kids?

"Pen, we have to stop. I'm your uncle, and you're underage."

She whines, rolling her hips and grinding against my length, the action making my balls draw up in anticipation. There's no doubt in my mind that if we kept dry humping like this, I'd end up coming in my pants.

Pen's breathing is labored, her lids heavy with desire. "But I don't want to stop."

I grip her jaw with one hand before pressing a hard kiss to her lips. "Trust me, baby. I don't want to stop either, but I can't keep doing this. I'm human and if we keep at it, I won't be able to stop. Not until my cock is buried deep inside that wet cunt, filling you up and making you mine."

Pen's body shudders at my words, her eyes twinkling with desire. "Yes, Daddy."

A deep chuckle rumbles through me, my head flinging back into the headrest. "You're seventeen, Pen. I can't. No matter how bad I want to, I can't."

Her lips purse to the side, her eyes narrowing on mine. "But if I weren't, then you'd take me? Make me yours?"

My dick twitches at her words, the movement causing Pen to squeal.

Digging my fingers into her hips, I give her a squeeze. "Princess, there isn't a man on this earth that could stop me."

A mischievous smile plays on her lips as she quirks a brow. "Well, just because you can't do anything doesn't mean I can't."

"Penelope," I warn, my voice coming out low and deliberate.

"What? You can't get into trouble if you're not doing anything." She grabs hold of my wrists, directing my hands behind my head and making them grip onto the headrest like she'd done before.

May god have mercy on my soul because the look in her eyes tells me she's got this all figured out and I don't stand a chance in hell. Which is perfect, because at this rate, I've bought myself a one-way ticket there.

Penelope

I'm nervous as hell, but I'm also on fire with need. It's like my whole body had been dormant, waiting for him to set it ablaze. All of my crazy teenage hormones were put on lockdown, only to have Jack set them free.

And now that they're out, there's no putting them back. My need for his body overpowers whatever reservations I have, making my hands travel down his arms and onto his chest. They explore the hard planes of his pecs, down the hard ridges of his abs, reveling in the gloriousness of his body. *God, he's delicious. So much hotter than the dumb guys at my prep school.*

"Don't move your hands. Remember. No touching, Daddy." Jack groans at my words, his length bumping against my ass as I slide off of him and onto the bench seat.

"Princess, this isn't a good idea. I'm a grown man. You shouldn't be touching me like this." There's pain in his eyes and the need to make it go away is visceral.

"I just want to make you feel good." My hands travel up his thighs and to his belt. I have no clue what I'm doing, but I've seen enough porn to get the gist of it. "Please, can I touch you? Can I put you in my mouth, Daddy?"

I know this game we're playing is sick. But I don't care. He's almost twice my age and my uncle, add to that this sinfully delicious role playing and it's enough to send most running for the hills. But me? I fucking love it. It makes every part of me light up with need. The need to make him cum. To make him happy. To make him whole.

His jaw clenches, but he closes his eyes and nods yes. Taking his permission and running with it, I undo his belt, lowering his pants as far as I can until he helps me by lifting himself closer to me and allowing me to take him out.

Pulling down his boxers, his hard flesh pops free, the mushroom tip tapping my lip in greeting. Jack groans and looking up, I see his eyes are trained on my mouth, his nostrils flaring in anticipation.

"Fuck, baby. You have no idea how many times I've thought about your pouty lips taking my fat cock. This is like a wet dream come true."

I whimper, the need to taste him overwhelming. With his eyes still on me, I hesitantly lick his bulbous head before taking it all in. Jack's legs shake and his breath shudders. Even though I'm inexperienced, I know I must be doing something right.

"I've never done this before." I poke my tongue out and give him another little lick. "Tell me what to do. Tell me what you need."

Jack's eyes narrow before closing, his chest rising and falling with a deep intake of breath. "Baby, you're not ready for what I need. What I need is to throw you over this bench seat, rip your little panties off and fuck you raw."

My whole body shivers, wanting the very thing he's just said.

His hand reaches for me but I stop him. "Naughty, Daddy. No touching. Only talking. Tell me what I can do to make you feel better." I grip his rigid flesh and give one hard pull before dropping my mouth over it and sucking him in as deep as I can go. Pressing my tongue to the underside, I ease back, slowly releasing him with a pop. "Does that help?"

I look up at him through hooded lids and see his clenched jaw and bared teeth. "Christ, Pen. I almost came down your throat. How can a sweet little virgin suck cock so good?"

His compliment makes my cheeks heat, encouraging me to keep going. Lowering myself back onto his flesh, I take his length deep; the action making me gag.

"That's right, baby. Swallow Daddy's big cock. Make me feel good." His words come out through gritted teeth, the filthiness of it all making my pussy tingle and clench.

I work myself up to his tip, swirling around his head before coming back down until he hits the back of my throat, and then I do as he asked. I swallow.

"Fuck. Fuck. Fuuuuck. Baby, that's right. Choke my cock with your sweet little throat." He's trying to hold himself as still as possible, the action making his entire body vibrate. "Jesus, you love Daddy's cock. Don't you, my dirty little girl?"

I whine around his length; the vibration making it jolt up and shove farther down my throat. I'm gagging, tears streaming down my face, but I'm so damn happy. I'm doing this to him. Making him so lost in our lust that he's giving in to me.

"Pull back, Princess. I don't want to hurt you, and god knows it's taking everything in me not to thrust into you like a wild animal."

I pull back, sucking in some much needed air, keeping one hand at his base and the other traveling down under my dress. I can't help it. I need to touch myself before I combust.

Jack's eyes track my movement, his pupils blowing out further and turning his hazel eyes black. "That's right, Princess. Lift that pretty dress and touch that needy pussy."

I do as he says, slowly trailing my hand up my leg before slipping my fingers under the cotton of my panties. Jack groans, dropping one of his hands over mine, his grip making me squeeze his cock harder. We both shudder, the forbidden nature of this making it so much hotter.

Painfully slow, he pumps our hands up and down his length, his eyes trained on where my other hand is. "Take your panties off, sweetheart. Show Daddy how wet and ready you are for him."

Doing the best I can with only one hand, I slide the panties off the rest of the way. I'm about to toss them onto the seat when Jack's other hand reaches out and grabs them.

My jaw drops open as he brings the wet spot to his nose, taking in a deep inhale. "Christ, Princess. You're so fucking ripe."

To my horror, his tongue pokes out, swiping at the drenched fabric. Unfazed, Jack moans in pleasure. "Mmmm. You taste so damn good, just like I knew you would."

He bucks once into our joint hands, his hand now moving harder and faster. Extending one of his legs onto the bench, he motions for me to get on. "I might not be able to touch right now, but I still need to make sure my little girl gets off. Get on and ride me, baby. Make that little wet cunt of yours feel good for Daddy."

Oh. My. God. Yes. This is so damn hot, I don't hesitate for a second.

Straddling his leg, I let my bare flesh grind on his jeans. The friction of the course material against my swollen nub makes me mewl in pleasure. God, this feels so damn good. I can't imagine what it would feel like to actually have him inside me.

"That's right, Princess. Ride Daddy's leg like the dirty little girl you are." He makes a choked sound, all while he continues to stroke his length with our hands.

I'm rocking back and forth on him, reveling in the sensation, but needing more. I need him inside me. Doing the only thing I can, I lower my mouth and suck on the tip of his cock, our hands coming up to meet my lips with every upward thrust.

"Fuck, baby. You're so damn beautiful like this. Sucking my cock while you get yourself off." He lets out a noise, his movements turning jerky. "God, I won't last much longer. Make yourself come, baby. Rub that little clit on Daddy."

His filthy words have my entire body tingling, the pleasure rocketing into a crescendo of sensation, making everything go black as I explode.

"Yes, baby. Take your pleasure. It's all yours." Jack grits out, the pumping of our hands never stopping. As soon as I've ridden out the last wave of pleasure, Jack's hands find my waist. He lifts me up and flips me onto my back on the bench seat. Before I know what's happening, he's lifting up my dress, exposing my core for the world to see.

"*Goddamnit.* You're so fucking perfect." He's sitting back on his heels, one hand gripping tightly onto his cock, pumping it with hard long tugs. "*Mine.* Those pouty pink lips are mine."

"Yours, Jack. All yours."

Jack releases a feral growl, his hand pumping violently as thick white ropes of cum spray across my mound, the evidence of his love trickling down my lips and teasing my already sensitive nub. I part my legs, showing him more of me, showing him just how dirty he's made me.

The skin around his eyes crinkles. "God, you're so filthy and I fucking love it. Never seen something so beautiful."

I'm burning up from his praise when the interior of the cab is lit up from behind. *Headlights.* Someone's pulled up behind us.

"Shit." Jack jerks my dress down and shoves my panties into his pocket before tucking himself back in.

He's lowered himself back into his seat, and the smolder that was in his eyes not two minutes ago has vanished. Despite his changed demeanor, the truck smells of sex and I have no doubt that as soon as that window lowers, our visitor will know exactly what we'd been up to.

FILTHY CROWN

Chapter Eighteen
JACK

ammit. I bet that's Ericson.

Great timing, buddy.

I need to get out of the truck before he knocks on the window. He may live all alone up here in the mountains, but he sure as fuck knows what sex smells like, and that's the last thing we need.

Pen's my niece, and even though we aren't blood, I don't want to risk this getting out and tarnishing her reputation or worse...the State trying to take her from me.

"Stay in the truck."

Pen rolls her eyes but does as she's told. Thank god. One look at her current state and I know I'll have to do some explaining. The back of Pen's hair is mussed, her face is flushed,

She looks damn edible.

Biting back a smile, I push the truck door open and step outside. Sure enough, I see my old college friend walking toward me.

"Jack? Is that you?"

"Sure is." I motion toward the truck. "Got stuck in some mud avoiding a doe. Thought we'd wait you out and see if you could help us get unstuck. We need to make it out to Hunter's cabin."

He cuts his gaze toward the truck, his eyes narrowing in on the passenger side. "We? Did the infamous bachelor finally land himself a missus?"

I let out a snort but then reign it back in as visions of Pen, barefoot and pregnant, hit me like a bat to the head. My knees go weak at the realization that the idea floods me with joy instead of terror, but that sensation quickly turns into horror as I realize the predicament it leaves us in.

It's not like I can have her... *can I?*

"Wow. Jack. Didn't mean to scare the shit out of you. You look like you've seen a ghost." He's right in front of me now, his hand reaching out and patting me on the shoulder. "I see you're still the same ol' Jack. Refusing to settle down then."

I blink away the thought of Pen carrying my baby and plaster on a smile. "Just the same ol' Jack here." Hitching a thumb toward the truck, I explain away the woman who's just shattered any preconceived notions I've had about relationships. With her, I want it all. "That's my niece. Austin's kids are living with me now."

Ericson's eyes go wide. There are very few reasons why a man's children would go to his brother, and none of them are good. "Shit. I'm sorry, man."

I give him a jerky nod, thankful he's not asking what happened. Now is definitely not the right time. "Thank you. Maybe on your day off you can drive down to the ranch, spend some time with the kids and the rest of our motley crew."

"I'd like that." He gives me a genuine smile before surveying the truck. "But first, we need to get you out of here."

"Sounds good. I think if you pull up in front of us, you'll be able to hitch us to your truck and pull us out."

"Yeah, I think you're right." He walks toward his truck, and I've never been so thankful in my life.

I'm glad Pen didn't disobey me and come out to say hello. Yes, it's rude, but I rather her be perceived as rude than Ericson catch wind of what we were up to. And I'm not going to lie. A part of me is also grateful he didn't see her because she's so damn beautiful. The thought of any other man seeing her and wanting to take her away sets free this rage filled panic I've never felt before, and frankly, it's unnerving.

That tiny woman holds so much power over me, and she doesn't even know it.

The crunching of snow and sloshing of mud has me looking away from my truck and toward Ericson. He's pulled up in front of us and is getting between our two vehicles, he's about to attach his chain to my tow hitch when his face transforms—his eyes go wide and lips spread into a shit-eating smile.

Fuck. He's seen her.

"Jack." He finally breaks his stare into the cab and looks toward me. "You didn't tell me Austin's little girl was all grown up."

Out of my periphery, I see Pen raise her hand and wiggle her fingers in greeting. "Hi! I'd come out, but it's colder than a witch's tit out there and I didn't dress for the occasion." She speaks through the glass and it comes out muffled but still audible.

Ericson turns back to her, his greedy eyes taking in all of her disheveled beauty, and it takes everything in me not to go physically turn his head away. *She's mine.*

Ericson's grin turns into a smirk. "I can see that. Shame on your uncle for not making sure you were prepared."

I narrow my eyes at him. "We were going down valley when we got a call from Hunter. He needed us to run him and my other brothers some gas."

My friend's brows come together. "That's not like Hunter. He's always prepared. When he first moved up here, I used to check on him all the time, and now we just meet up once a month to shoot the shit." He shakes his head and laughs. "I swear, that man is better equipped to tackle the outdoors than I am."

I smile. "That sounds like him. And yes, he typically is." I look toward Pen and lower my voice, not wanting her to hear. "Someone syphoned out the gas from all of their vehicles and I'm guessing his reserve tank as well."

Ericson's smile falls at my words. "Damn. I really do need to catch up with y'all. Come on. Let's get you out of here and I'll follow you to his cabin. Doesn't hurt to have backup or a fresh set of eyes."

I nod, but internally I'm shouting '*Hell. No.*'

The more time we spend together, the more time he has to

figure something isn't right between Pen and me. Hell, I haven't even properly had her and I already feel possessive as a motherfucker. There's no hiding that.

He rounds the truck and is about to turn to his driver's side door when he stops in his tracks, his face turning red. "You might want to tuck that back in."

I look down to my fly in horror, but then downright black out when I see what he was pointing at. Pen's little white thong is sticking out of my pocket, the lace detailing leaving no room for interpretation. It's a fucking thong in my pocket and the only female around is my niece.

My vision blurs as I step back into the truck, Pen's voice echoing in my head and sounding like a Charlie Brown cartoon. It isn't until she's physically shaking me that I come out of my stupor.

"Jack. Push on the gas." Her slender fingers dig into my shoulder, moving me into action.

The truck jerks forward, and I've finally gained some traction. Once I've maneuvered us onto the road, I let Pen in on our predicament. Taking out the panties, I clench them in front of her. "He knows."

She sucks in a sharp breath, her body flushing pink. "It's okay, right? He's your friend. It's not like you made me do anything."

I shove the white fabric back into my pocket, clenching my jaw and gritting out words I wish I could take back as soon as I say them. "It's wrong, Pen. You know it. I know it. And now *he* knows it. What we did is sick and wrong."

Her eyes well up and I feel like the biggest jackass on the

planet. She wipes away at a tear, looking out the window and refusing to give me her gaze. "It didn't feel wrong."

She's right. What we did in this truck felt like the farthest thing from wrong. It was right in every way that mattered. Never in my life had I felt that connected to a woman, needing her to find pleasure was my only driving source. Whatever pleasure I received came secondary.

Don't get me wrong, I always made sure my partners got their rocks off, but the ultimate game plan was about my enjoyment. But not with Pen. It was all about her, what made her feel good, what made her breath hitch and cheeks flush.

God, I could get used to seeing her like that every day, splayed out and ready to take me. A knock on the window pulls me from my thoughts, and I roll it down. Knowing there's no sense in hiding the obvious scent. He knows full well what we were doing to pass the time.

"I've unhooked your truck. The roads should be clear but I'll follow y'all up there just to make sure you get to the boys safely." His expression is serious, not a friendly smile to be had. That's fine. I don't need anyone but my family, and as long as he doesn't make moves to take Pen away, then we won't have any problems.

With a dip of my head, I give him my thank you before rolling up my window as he retreats to his truck.

Pen lets out a snort. "Oh, he definitely knows."

"Yup." The one word is all I can muster, my head swimming with dreadful thoughts of Pen leaving. Reaching out, I give her thigh a squeeze. "Don't worry, Princess. Everything's going to be okay."

And I mean it. I'll do whatever I have to in order to make sure she stays with me. There isn't a man on this earth that could pry her away.

Chapter Nineteen
PENELOPE

I can fix this. I just need to get Ericson alone and explain to him that this is none of his business. Mentally psyching myself to talk to a complete stranger about my sexual escapade with Jack is not something I thought I'd be doing today, but here I am. I need to do this.

Jack is right. If Ericson feels what's going on between Jack and me is wrong, he can report us and then I'll be taken away. I can't let that happen. Not only because I want to leave on my own terms but because it would traumatize Amanda and Alex to see someone else they love leave them like that.

We've been winding up the mountain for a while and even though it's dark, I can see why Hunter likes it up here. There's nothing but wilderness and the idea of being surrounded by nothing but nature is extremely appealing.

After going around another bend, the truck veers into a path cutting deeper into the mountain.

"We're here." Jack announces while looking out the windshield. He hasn't looked at me since we first took off and I can only imagine what's going on inside of his gorgeous head.

The thicket of trees clears and gives way to a small clearing where a substantial sized cabin sits. Wow. It's stunning. I thought his home would be a little more rugged than this, but it's like a larger version of the cabin by the waterfall.

Same massive windows adorn the home and I can only imagine how this place looks in the winter, sitting on one of the couches and staring out into the blanket of white powdery snow.

The truck comes to a complete stop, signaling it's time to face the music. Jack gives me one quick glance before assuring me once again that everything is going to be alright. "Don't worry, Pen. I can see the wheels turning in your head. It'll be fine."

I chuckle. "You didn't talk to me the entire ride up here and you've managed to read my mind how?"

His eyes focus on me, narrowing just a touch. "I know you, Princess. I studied your every facial expression for five years, watching for any signs of distress caused by the new relationship your mom had formed with my brother. You were this little spitfire with such a big heart, and I couldn't stand the idea of anything tarnishing that." His eyes cut to Ericson who's getting out of his truck. "I've always loved you, Pen. Maybe not always like this. *Definitely not like this.* But my heart loved you just the same."

Before I can say anything in response, Jack is opening his

door and stepping outside. I'm left sitting there in a daze at his words. Was that a declaration that he loves me now? Romantically?

Loud boisterous men cut into my thoughts and I see that Jace and Matt are pouring out of the cabin, both surrounding Ericson with warm greetings. It looks like they all know each other. Good. Hopefully, this will help my cause, and let him see I'm not in any danger and definitely don't need any rescuing.

I'm staring at the men when my door flings open and Jack is standing there, holding out a hand to me. "You coming, Princess?"

His words make me flush, remembering my coming on his pant leg. My eyes quickly dart to the area, making me heat even further. It isn't until Jack's clearing his throat that I realize his friend is staring straight at us. *Right.* I need to get on with my plan.

Taking Jack's hand, I step out of the truck and toward the rest of my uncles. As soon as I'm within range, each one surrounds me with a bear hug. "Ease up guys. I can barely breathe," I muffle through their various limbs.

"But we missed you," Jace teases. "How's Stalin treating you? Still giving you shit about your coffee?"

Jack grumbles behind me. "It's unnatural. Nobody should drink it cold unless they have to."

Ericson releases a snort, making my heart flutter with hope. Maybe he'll see things our way.

Untangling myself from the group hug, I face Jack before answering. "Jack has his moments, but I wouldn't want to be with anyone else. Even if he doesn't agree with my choice of coffee."

Matt grabs at his chest, "Not even your Uncle Matt?"

Jack growls, but I simply laugh. "And be subjected to the parade of women you'll bring around? No thanks." I tap him on the chest and make my way toward Hunter's front door.

"Where's Hunter?" Ericson asks.

Matt grimaces. "He's out checking the perimeter. Been doing that a lot since we arrived. Didn't take the news about Austin well. The guy blames himself like there was a way he could've stopped Austin from—"

Jack elbows his brother, cutting off his words. "Watch it."

All three men turn to look at me, Matt's lips turning down in a frown. "I'm sorry, Pen."

I raise my hands, palms up. "Hey, there's no need to treat me like a fragile princess. Besides, Ericson here doesn't know the full story. We should probably fill him in."

My eyes cut back to the park ranger, trying to convey that I'm fine. His eyes meet mine and I can see that worry lurks behind them. I'm just not sure if it's for me or for what happened with Austin.

Maybe it's a little of both.

"Let's get Pen inside. It's too cold for her out here." Jack sidles up to me, his muscular arm pulling me into his side in a protective manner, making me melt a little inside.

'Definitely not like this.' His words from earlier come to mind and I wonder if the love he has for me now is the kind that a man has for a woman, not a little girl.

Matt coughs awkwardly, his eyes darting back and forth between Jack and me. "Right. Pen, you must be freezing. Let's get you inside."

Jace chimes in from ahead as we all walk toward the cabin. "Yes. What on earth would possess you to wear that little dress up here?"

Jack snorts while I roll my eyes and groan. "I thought we were going down valley."

Something tells me I'll never live this wardrobe choice down.

Stepping out of the cold and into the cabin, I'm surrounded by warmth. My eyes fall on a massive fireplace, roaring with a fire in the hearth. Immediately, I plant my butt on the chair closest to it, enjoying the heat it provides.

Not two seconds later, a blanket is being placed around my shoulders and a kiss is being pressed to my head. "Get warm, Princess. I need to talk to the guys real quick." Looking behind me, I see Jack's worried expression.

Matt coughs again, making me turn. He's got this funny look on his face I can't quite place. It's a cross between constipation and choking. I'm about to say something when Jack cuts me off. "Matt, Jace, I need a minute with you. Ericson, if you don't mind keeping an eye on Pen. I don't want to leave her alone." He looks out into the dark night and a shiver runs through me. *Am I still in danger?* "As soon as I'm done talking to the guys, we'll fill you in on everything."

Ericson's eyes are narrowed on Jack, and despite whatever he might be thinking, he gives Jack a nod before coming to sit in the chair directly across from mine. "She's safe *with me*."

There's an edge to his voice that would indicate I'm not safe with Jack and he doesn't miss it. Jace, not being one who's comfortable with awkward tension, cuts in. "Alright, let's get this party started so we can all get down to the ranch. My stomach is mad at me for letting it put up with Hunter's culinary skills and I can sure use some of Mary's home cooking right now."

"Don't talk about Mary's cooking right now. I'm serious when I say I dream about that woman's roast." Matt's stomach grumbles and we all chuckle, ending the strange tension if just for a moment.

With Matt's plea, all three Crown brothers disappear into a hallway, leaving Ericson and me alone.

As soon as the men aren't within earshot, I turn to my current guard. "Listen, I know what you're probably thinking, but the reality is far from it." He chokes back a snort, but I ignore it and continue. "My mother worked two jobs and went to night school. I don't even remember my dad. My point is I had to learn how to fend for myself from a very young age and I can tell the difference between someone taking advantage, abusing, or genuinely caring."

Ericson's face turns red, "But you're so—"

I hold up a finger, cutting him off. "I'm not done. Because if all that wasn't enough, within the last month I've been abducted by a cartel, held in dismal conditions for a week, and watched my mother be raped and decapitated in front of my very eyes."

"Jesus." Ericson's face turns green at my words.

"My mother's dying wish was that I look after my little brother and sister, who also bore witness to her suffering. As you already know, Jack is our guardian and if you so much as hint at any mistreatment by him, including whatever you think you know is happening between the two of us, then you'll not only tarnish your friendship with him but you'll also be making sure I'm torn away from my little brother and sister. That would traumatize them further and you'd be making me break my promise to our mother."

Ericson swallows hard. "I see…"

"So please, I politely ask that you keep any thoughts to yourself and stay out of our business."

A clearing of someone's throat has me whipping my head around and I come face to face with a towering lumberjack. Hunter's muscular six-foot-three frame is standing behind my chair, an unreadable look on his face.

"Hunter!" I squeak, jumping out of my seat and wrapping my arms around him in a hug.

Despite Jack staying away these past four years, Hunter visited us at least twice a year. He may be a recluse, but he's a consistent and dependable recluse.

His brawny arms wrap around me, his chest vibrating with his words. "Hey shrimp." He looks over my head and nods at his friend. "Ericson. Where are they?"

"Hello to you too, asshole." Ericson shakes his head, but the smile on his face says this is normal for them. "They went that way. Said they had to discuss something before they fill me in on what happened." He drops his gaze to me still in Hunter's arms. "But I think your shrimp here filled me in on everything I need to know."

Hunter nods his head twice, his face as stoic as ever. Finally releasing his hold on me, he walks toward the hallway. "I'll be back."

"A man of few words." I chuckle awkwardly at Ericson. Now that I've said my peace, I don't know what else to do but wait out the Crown men.

Seeing a chessboard on the console table, I make a truce offering. "Up for a game?"

FILTHY CROWN

Chapter Twenty
JACK

"**W**hat the hell was that?" Matt is pacing back and forth, never once taking his eyes off me.

"What was what?" My brows push together, wondering what in the world he's talking about.

"The way you're looking and touching Pen. It's a little too…" Matt's words cut off, but Jace chimes in.

"Friendly." His tone is teasing, unlike Matt's serious one.

My fists ball up, unsure of what to tell them. It's not like I'm going to come out and tell them what just happened in my truck.

"*Oh god.* What have you done, Jack?" Matt stops his pacing and is looking at me head on, all while Jace bares an amused expression.

"What I do or don't do with Pen is none of your business.

Last I checked, she was living under my roof." I cross my arms and puff out my chest. I may not know what the hell I'm going to do about our situation, but the last thing I'll allow is for anyone to shame us.

"Are you out of your goddamn mind?!" Matt whisper-hisses through his teeth.

"Never been clearer. I asked you here so we could talk about our plan of action with the cartel, not so we could discuss Pen and me."

"Jesus. So it's true? There's a '*Pen and you*'?" Matt's eyes practically bulge out while Jace snickers, making Matt turn to him. "And you? What the hell is wrong with you? This is so damn wrong. It's sick. Jack could get into so much trouble."

Jace finally turns serious. "First, you don't know *what,* if anything, has happened between the two of them. Second, have you been around those two? I mean with your eyes open, because if you had, then you would've seen this coming a mile away. The tension between those two is insane. They either would've ended up killing each other or fucking. Frankly, I'm glad it's the latter and not the former."

Matt stands there slack jawed, as do I. Is this thing I have for Pen that damn obvious that my fun-loving brother saw it clearly?

Matt finally gathers his wits and points a finger into Jace's chest. "What happens when that girl turns on him? When she decides to tell the authorities that it *wasn't* mutual? Are you willing to lose one more Crown brother because of a Garcia woman?"

Jace sucks in a sharp breath, his eyes narrowing into tiny

slits. I'm about to set Matt straight when Hunter cuts in. "I don't think that'll be a problem."

We all turn to look at Matt with raised brows. "Oh, yeah? And what makes you so sure of that?"

Hunter graces us with a rare smile, unusual for the stoic man. "The fact that she just reamed out Ericson for even thinking of Jack in a negative light and basically guilted him into keeping quiet. That's what."

Matt's mouth hangs open while Jace and I both grin. Pen is feisty and strong. She's perfect.

I'm grinning like a fool, proud of my strong-willed girl. Meanwhile, Matt has both hands in his hair and tugging at the ends. "Ericson knows? How are you not worried about this, Jack?

"Based on what Hunter said, seems to me like Pen handled it. I'll still talk to him and make sure he knows I haven't touched her, but I'm not worried about it." My face is devoid of emotion. I mean what I say. Whatever comes my way as a result, I'll handle it. Pen is worth that and so much more.

"So you *haven't* touched her? There's nothing going on between the two of you?" Matt's brows push together while the other two Crown brothers stand back, looking bored.

"Like I said, what I do and don't do with Pen is none of your business. All you need to know is that I would never hurt her. I'd never force her to do something she didn't want to, and I sure as hell wouldn't do anything that would make her feel uncomfortable. Especially not after what those fuckers did to her." My face grows heated at the memory of her body trembling in my arms as she recounted her experience in

Mexico.

"Speaking of which," Hunter interrupts my tiff with Matt, effectively ending it and moving us on to the reason I brought them back here in the first place. "I think they're the ones who messed with our gas tanks and my reserves."

I nod. "I have the same suspicion, though I don't understand why they'd take the gas instead of slashing tires."

Jace jumps in, "It takes longer to syphon gas than it does to slit tires. I think they wanted us to know that they took their sweet time, right under our noses and we hadn't the faintest clue. Sort of like showing us what they're capable of doing and what they're going to try next."

My fists ball up and my body goes taut. "Over my dead body. Those assholes have another thing coming if they think they'll take Pen and the kids."

Matt cocks a brow, his lip curling up in a sneer. "I see you're not lumping Pen into the kid category anymore."

I roll my eyes and shake my head. Truth is, I stopped doing that as soon as I saw her exit the WRATH securities vehicle. One look at her and you know she's all woman. Even the way she carries herself exudes more maturity than Georgina, a woman ten years her senior. Sure, she has her moments of stubbornness, but that's something women Mary's age still do.

"Enough," I growl at Matt. "We need to focus on the threat, so stop picking at me and Pen. *That's* none of your business."

Jace speaks up, turning toward Matt. "You asked me if I wanted another Crown brother falling to a Garcia woman. Do you think that what happened in Mexico was Blanca's fault?"

All of our eyes train on Matt, this new tidbit of information intriguing. "I'd been doing some digging. I think it was our brother's wife who introduced him to the cartel."

My head rears back, but it's Hunter who speaks up. "And what makes you think that?"

"I looked into her background. She was born in the same town as one of Las Cruces rival cartels. She could've, I don't know, known someone and introduced them to Austin."

My nostrils flare as I take a step forward and get into Matt's face. "Are you fucking kidding me right now? All you have is the fact that Pen's mom was Mexican, and *that's* what you're using to pin Austin's actions on her? I'll ask you what you asked me. Have you lost *your* goddamn mind, brother?"

Matt's jaw clenches, his body standing still, refusing to back down. "It's a gut feeling, Jack. I know she's tied into this somehow."

I shake my head in disbelief. "Even if she had something to do with it, that has nothing to do with Pen. And you're over here concocting stories in your head, meanwhile we have a real security threat that needs to be dealt with."

Jace slaps Matt on the back. "I agree with Jack. We need to be focusing on keeping the kids safe while the men of WRATH continue their investigation."

Hunter turns to me. "So what's the plan?"

"All of you are coming back to the ranch and staying with us. The more eyes on them, the better. As soon as we get back home, we can talk to the men of WRATH and see if they've found anything new. Anything we can use to secure Pen and the kids' safety."

My brothers all nod in agreement. Thank fuck, because I was

prepared to drag them all back if I had to.

Matt places his hand on my shoulder, his fingers digging into my traps. "I'm coming back with you and I'll be keeping a close eye on you and Pen. Make no mistake, if you step out of line, I'll beat your ass."

Hunter outright snorts, an unusual expression for our brother. "You do that and you'll be hearing from Pen. I can assure you of that. That girl has no qualms with putting people in their place when it comes to whatever that is." Hunter waves his hand toward me.

His words have a sense of pride warming my chest. Despite the murky waters Pen and I are in, she's still standing up for us.

"Alright. So how are we doing this?" Jace raises a brow, waiting on an answer.

"I say we take all of the vehicles. Hunter, take as much as you can because you aren't leaving the ranch until this is over. I can put you in one of our cabins if the main house is too much." Hunter nods, so I continue. "As for Ericson, I think I need to have a talk with him and fill him in personally. Even though Pen talked to him, I want to make sure there's no animosity."

Matt chortles. "You mean you don't want him reporting your ass."

I let out a tired breath. "That too. Alright, let's get to it."

Dismissing my brothers, I turn toward the door and my awkward as hell conversation with Ericson. One of many to come, I'm sure. Despite what I told Pen in the car, she isn't a mistake.

I want everything with her. She's mine. Now that I know

what she tastes like, there's not a man on this earth who could keep me from her. The only thing left is to figure out the logistics. Do I stay away until she's ready for me? Let her live her life without me, or do I selfishly insert myself and refuse to let her leave my side?

God, this is all too much. Taking it one step at a time, I head toward my old friend. Keeping a lid on him is priority number one.

Awkward emotions are an afterthought as soon as I catch sight of Pen and Ericsson, laughing over a game of chess, his hand resting dangerously close to hers.

The air shifts as soon as I step beside the two. "Well, aren't we cozy?"

Pen looks up from the board, her face scrunching in question. "Jack?"

"Yeah, *Jack*." Ericson raises a brow, begging me to give him shit for what I rationally know was nothing at all. But does my brain listen to ration right now? Hell no. All it knows is that it needs to get this man away from my Pen.

"Ericson. Outside." I turn and head toward the door, not waiting for a response.

As I'm stepping out, I hear my old friend grumble as my brothers chuckle apologies for my behavior. Whatever. Just wait until they find the one that makes them lose all coherent thought. I'll be the first to point it out.

Once outside, Ericson's eyes narrow on mine. "Look, Jack.

I have no damn clue what's going on between you and that girl—"

"That's right, you don't. And despite whatever you think you saw, I can assure you that I would never hurt her."

Ericson holds his palms up. "If you'd let me finish…" I nod, and he continues. "I have no clue what's going on between you two, and at the first inkling that she's being taken advantage of, I'll be the first one to beat the ever-loving shit out of you…"

I growl, taking a step toward him and fisting his shirt up before walking him back into a wall. "Be careful with what you say next, friend. That girl in there is my world and if you threaten what I have with her, it'll be the end of you."

Ericson chuckles, even as I'm pinning him to the wall. "Like I was saying, if I see that, then I'll have no problem stepping up. But from what I see, she's a strong-willed young woman and you have your hands full."

I drop my grip and take a step back, narrowing my eyes. "So what are you saying?"

"I don't condone it. Whatever it is you have with a girl so young she could be your daughter. But different strokes for different folks, I suppose. She seems to have a good head on her shoulders and she sure as hell doesn't seem like a little pushover you could bend to your will." He laughs, shaking his head. "Good luck, brother. Like I said, you're going to have your hands full."

A grin splits my face, and heartfelt words are spilling out of me before I can hold them back. "Yeah, but I don't mind. If I play my cards right, she'll keep me on my toes until the day I die."

Ericson's brows raise. "Wow. It's that serious?" I nod, while the look of shock settles on his face. "Damn. Who'd have thought that Austin's stepdaughter would've been the one to bring you to your knees."

"Definitely not me. I still don't know what the hell this is or what we're going to do. She's so young and I don't want to hold her back in any way. All I know is that I care for her more than I should, and if loving her means letting her go live her life, then that's what I'll do." I'm running a hand over my face, wondering how in the hell I ended up here. Falling hard for a damn teenager. As if in answer, visions of my brother flash before me. *Austin, that's how.* "But before we can even start figuring all that out, we have to deal with a very real threat. I'm not sure how much Penelope told you, but my brother and his family were abducted in Mexico. We're still working on getting all of the information, but it looks like he was doing business with the Las Cruces cartel."

Ericson blows out a low whistle. "Wow. I would've never pegged him for following in his daddy's footsteps."

I raise a brow. "So Hunter filled you in on his theories about that?"

Ericson nods. "Sure did. Said your old man was doing business with those fuckers. But with what happened with your parents, why on earth would Austin go and stir that hornet's nest? Just doesn't make sense."

"Your guess is as good as mine. We have a team looking into it, but for now, all we know is that they took them and held them for a week. We were able to retrieve Pen and the kids, but it was too late for my brother and his wife." My head drops back and I curse at life for being so damn cruel.

"Christ. Those poor kids. A whole week held by those assholes. I can't even imagine."

"Yes, and now we think they're here. Wanting to tie up loose ends." My eyes flit back inside to where Pen is smiling up at Hunter as he shakes his head. I love that she's close to my brothers. She'll always be protected here. Safe. "That's why I need you to monitor Hunter's property. He'll be coming down with us and staying at the ranch until everything's settled. I'm not sure if they'll try to come back up here, but we could sure use an extra set of eyes."

"Of course. He's like family. You all are. Even you with your perverted ass ways." He's laughing and I'm glaring.

"What I have with Pen is far from perverted, asshole. Sure, there's a physical component to it, but I'm drawn to her fire. Despite the shit hand life has dealt her, she makes the most of it, and all while being fiercely loyal and protective over those she loves. I'm in awe of her. Always have been, but now that she's a woman, it's different. It's like a veil has been lifted and I see her in a completely different light." My eyes are focused on the silhouette of her face when I get a shove from Ericson.

"Look at you getting all emotional. This girl has turned you into a pussy." He's grinning, eyes dancing with mirth and I know I'll never live this down. The funny part is, I don't care.

"Ha. Ha. Get your laughs in. You'll get it when it finally happens to you."

"Yeah, well, that's not happening up here. Not unless by some miracle the woman of my dreams can be found on one of my hiking trails." He shivers before turning to walk back inside.

"Let's get this show on the road. Temp's dropping and I need to get back to the station."

The wind howls as if in agreement, and it's all fine with me. The sooner we get going, the sooner we're all back home where it's safe.

Chapter Twenty-One
PENELOPE

"P en!" A little blonde whirl of emotions comes barreling into me, followed by our solemn brother, Alex.

"Hey, guys." I crouch down, pulling them both into my arms. "What happened? What's wrong?"

Amanda pulls back enough so she can see my face, her big green eyes wet with tears. "You left, and you were gone for so long."

"We thought you weren't coming back," Alex whispers into my hair.

Jesus. My heart. It feels like it's breaking into a million little pieces.

"No, guys," I squeeze them tighter. "I'd never leave you. I

I know that's not something I should do. Nobody could promise forever. But hearing their words full of so much raw fear and sadness, I can't help and indulge. It's not like I have any intention of leaving them anyway. They'd have to pry me from them and even then, I'd find a way to come back.

"It's late, but how about we let your sister change and then she can meet us in the study for some hot chocolate." Jack is ruffling Alex's hair, his hand outstretched to Amanda.

She's beaming up at him, batting her lashes. "Can we have whipped cream and marshmallows too?"

Jack chuckles, "Of course. Let's go ask Mary where she's hiding them."

"Behind the oatmeal," Jace offers, making Matt snort.

"Of course you'd know where the marshmallows are." He's shaking his head when the kids finally release their death grip around me.

I don't mind the love and affection. In fact, I soak up every second of it. Tomorrow isn't promised, and forever isn't real. But Jack is right, I need to change.

Since I had no panties, I ended up wiping off his spend with the underside of my dress. To say that I'm uncomfortable would be an understatement.

Though the thought of walking around marked by Jack is appealing, I'd really like a hot bath right about now. Pressing a kiss to both kids' heads, I give them my promise that I'll join them soon. "Save me some marshmallows. Don't let Uncle Jace eat them all."

Amanda giggles while Alex is stone cold serious. "I promise, Pen."

My little man. He's such a good brother. I just hope that everything we've been through hasn't scarred him for life.

With a sigh, I turn and walk up the stairs, taking them two at a time. There's a walk-in shower that's calling my name.

A wicked thought springs to mind as soon as I hit the landing. I have no freaking clue what Jack and I are, if we're anything at all, but seeing as how I'm still covered in him, he shouldn't begrudge me getting cleaned up in his bath.

He has a massive walk-in shower that doubles as a sauna and I could definitely use a steam right about now. The fear of not knowing if the cartel threat is still alive and well gives me a bone-deep chill.

Even now, as I step into his room, a shiver wracks through me. His room is so masculine, in deep shades of gray and white. It's stunning. My eyes land on his king-sized bed, decked out in this cloud like comforter that begs to be jumped on.

Shaking my head, I walk toward the shower. That's where I'm going, not his bed.

Stepping into the all white space, I turn the shower on and hit the dials for the sauna. I'm so excited I can barely stand still. I'm about to start stripping when I realize I haven't brought anything with me, and despite what Jack and I did in his truck, I still don't feel comfortable walking out of his room in just a towel. I'd be mortified if his brothers or Mary saw me.

Leaving the water running and the shower steaming up, I turn and open the door to the bedroom, my entire body freezing at the vision before me.

A buck ass naked woman is lying on Jack's bed. Legs spread wide for me to see. "What the actual fuck, Georgina!" I shriek, my voice coming out like some daemon possessed serpent. Red is all I see. This bitch must've thought it was Jack in the shower.

Oh my god. Does this mean they do this regularly?

I'm still standing at the bathroom entry frozen when the bedroom door flings open and men pour in. All four brothers stop at the foot of Jack's bed, their eyes in various states of surprise.

It's not until Jace cackles that Jack speaks. "What are you doing, Georgina?"

This bitch finally has the decency to cover up with a silk robe she must've brought with her. "I... I thought it was you in the shower."

All eyes fall on me, the bathroom entryway behind me as steam billows out all around me. I give them all a sheepish smile. "I wasn't feeling good, so I was going to use the sauna." I hitch my thumb back, as if it's the most normal thing in the world to use your uncle's shower instead of your own.

Jack blinks a couple of times before his eyes travel down my body, undressing me with his eyes. A full blush comes over me, the heated moment only being broken by Matt's growling and shoving of Jack.

Jack looks back toward Georgina, his brows pushing together. "I think this goes without saying, but I'll make it clear just the same. This is extremely unprofessional, Georgina. I don't know what gave you the impression that this," he waves a hand over her. "whatever this is, is okay. I've done nothing to ever give you the impression that I like to shit where I eat." Jace snickers and Matt grumbles, but Jack continues. "Frankly, this lack of judgment is not acceptable, and I can't have that around

Pen and the kids. You're terminated. I'll give you until tomorrow to collect your things and leave. You'll be given a severance package and that should be enough to get you wherever you need to go, but you're no longer welcome here."

"But Jack, I just wanted to make you feel good. You carry so much stress on your shoulders, I wanted to alleviate it."

My body is vibrating with rage. The irony that I told Jack pretty much the same thing not twenty-four hours ago also isn't lost on me. It's taking everything in me to not claw her face off. He's mine. Jack is mine. Only I get to make him feel good.

Is he though? Is he really yours? A little voice in the back of my head fights my anger, trying to inject logic into my emotions, but I'm not having it.

With clenched fists, I take a couple of steps toward her, ready to enact my kind of rationale. I've almost reached her when Hunter's strong arms come around me, pulling me back into his chest. "No, Princess. Let Jack handle this."

Jack's eyes cut to Hunter and then drop to where his arms are, the realization pulling a growl from his lips.

Georgina notices and releases a cackle that is so disturbing it belongs in a horror movie. "Oh, so that's what this is? You don't want a real woman, you want a little girl and I'm not young enough for you."

My face goes red as Jack's jaw clenches. "What I need is not your concern, Georgina. All you need to know is that you're no longer welcome here."

She sniffs, flicking her hair off her shoulder. "It doesn't take a rocket scientist to see she was using *your* shower, and the look on her face says she's jealous of all this and what you could have if only you'd let yourself."

My body jolts forward, reacting to her taunts, but Hunter keeps me held back firmly against his chest.

The room is quiet, nobody daring to confirm or deny any of her accusations. Georgina raises a brow as she gets off the bed and saunters over to Jack. "Go on and deny it. Tell me you feel nothing for that little girl. That it's all a one-sided crush. Some sick teenager lusting after her uncle." She turns to me, a wicked smile playing on her lips. "Because she is only seventeen, and you're far too old for her. It's practically illegal. Oh wait, it actually is."

Jack snarls. "Pen is my niece. Nothing more. She's a child and your accusations are fucking sick. Now, get the fuck out of my room and pack up your shit before I throw you out right this second."

His words sting, gouging deep fissures in my chest. I feel myself crumble against Hunter, his arms the only thing keeping me upright. Logic tells me he's lying, but just like before, my mind pays it no mind and my heart takes his words as truth.

"Mark my words, Jack. This is going to come back and bite you in the ass. You should've taken me while you had the chance." Georgina walks past the brothers, not sparing me another glance. Fine by me because I have no fight left.

Jack's words cut me down, taking me back to the rejected little girl waiting by the window for a man who never came. But I suppose that's what I was made for. Leaving. I owe that nugget of truth to my father. The very first man to ever let me down, and apparently not the last.

FILTHY CROWN

Chapter Twenty-Two

PENELOPE

Damp hair sticks to the back of my neck as I walk into Jack's study. After Georgina's production, I ended up heading back to my own shower. Hunter tried to soothe the sting of Jack's words by suggesting the sauna again, but at that point, it was just too awkward.

The guys ended up filing out and I walked back to my room, like a walk of shame with none of the fun that comes beforehand.

"Shhh." Jack shushes me as I come closer to Amanda and Alex, little bundles cuddled into each other. Both with hot chocolate mustaches.

"They look so sweet like this. I wish I had my phone so I could take a picture." Jack gets up, leaving his cozy chair by the

"Here. I'd like to get it printed and framed, that way we can both have it." His fingers touch mine and a zap of energy courses through the connection. Instantly, our eyes meet and so much emotion passes through them I'm left speechless.

Seconds pass before Jack clears his throat. "Once you're done with that, I'll take them up to their rooms."

I'm pulling up the camera app when I hear Matt's voice behind me, startling me to the point where I almost drop the phone.

"Jace and I can take them up," Matt grumbles. Turning around, I see that they were sitting by the door. *How did I miss them?*

This entire day has been a blur. I'm so out of sorts between what happened in the truck, the possibility of danger still lurking, and the whole Georgina debacle.

Pulling up the camera app again, I snap a couple of pictures, smiling at my favorite ones. Pointing at the last one I took, I turn to Jack, "Please print this one for me. They look so sweet cuddled up like this."

Jack pulls the phone with Jace and Matt flanking either side of him. "Wow. Alex looks so much like his dad here."

"They both do. But mom…"

Jack reaches out a hand, the back of his fingers running along my jawline. "You look like her. She lives on through you."

A tear falls, and Jack swiftly wipes it away with the pad of his thumb. "I'm so sorry, Princess."

"We all are," Matt speaks up, before scooping up Alex.

Jace nods, picking up Amanda and following behind his brother. "See you in the morning, peanut."

"Yes, maybe we can go for a ride. The kids would love that." I smile, remembering how much Amanda and Alex loved the horses.

"Only if it's close to the house." Jack raises a brow and both brothers nod in agreement before stepping out of the study.

I'm standing there, looking after them, when Jack's deep voice rumbles behind me. "Hot chocolate."

Turning around, I see him holding a mug, the warm glow of the fire illuminating his broad frame.

Taking it from his hands, I marvel at how there's still steam coming from the top. "Oh, wow. It's still warm."

"It's the mugs. They're insulated. We didn't know how long you'd be, so I had Mary use the ones we use around campfires." He looks from me to the couch, worry darkening his features. "Please sit. We need to talk."

Oh, god. That's never good. Wanting to get this over with, I do as he says and sit to the edge of the leather chesterfield sofa.

Instead of returning to his chair, Jack takes the seat beside me, our legs almost touching. "First, we need to figure out child care."

"What do you mean?" My brows push together, unsure of what he's getting at. "I'll watch over Amanda and Alex. It's my job and the only solace I could give mom before they took her from us. I promised her I would always look out for her babies and I don't have any plans on backing out of that."

A look of understanding flashes through his eyes. "Is that why you don't want to go to college? Because Pen, trust me when I say this, your mom would want what's best for you. She wouldn't want you to sacrifice yourself when there are other viable options for the kids."

He takes my free hand in his, interlocking our fingers and stealing my words. "Pen, I'm here. I'll watch over them as if they were my own. You don't have to worry about them."

"But I promised…" My words die in my throat. Truth is, even if I hadn't, there's no way I could leave those two behind. They're my little nuggets. I've been with them since the day they were born. They need me, just like I need them.

"Look, I was thinking. Mary has a granddaughter that comes to visit for the summers. She's been coming for the last couple of years and is scheduled to be here in two weeks. I'm thinking of offering her the live-in nanny position. She's got a good head on her shoulders and her stay here could give you enough time to get to know her. You'd be able to tell me if you felt good enough about her watching the kids while you go to college."

Removing my hands from his, I grip them tightly around the mug. "I already told you. I'm not going to college. And it's all good and well that Mary's granddaughter is visiting, she's probably lovely. But that doesn't change the fact that I'm not leaving those kids."

Jack takes my mug and places it on the console table behind the couch before fully facing me, his hands reaching out and grabbing mine. "Penelope, I can't stand by and let you sacrifice your future. You are brilliant. You've been awarded a full ride at an Ivy League school, for fuck's sake. That's no small feat. You can't throw that away because of some false sense of duty."

"False sense?!" I gasp, trying to pull my hands free, but Jack only holds them tighter, pulling me closer so that I'm practically on his lap. Anger mixes with lust and my entire body is set ablaze. "There is nothing fake about what I'm feeling."

Jacks' nostrils flare, his jaw clenching as he pulls me closer. "Are we still talking about the kids? Or is this about us?"

My chest is now on his, rising and falling with our agitated breaths. "The kids," I hiss, remembering his words from earlier. "There is no us."

Jack growls, his hands traveling up my arms until his grip is tightening around my biceps.

"Say that again and mean it, Princess." His eyes are boring into mine, searching for the truth.

"It doesn't matter if I mean it or not. You clearly don't see me as anything more than a kid."

Jack scoffs, his head falling back as he laughs, exposing the corded muscles of his neck and making me want to trail my tongue up the pulsing vein. With little thought, that's just what I do, the salty masculine taste of him exploding on my tongue upon contact.

"*Princess.*" Jack groans, grabbing me by the hips and dragging me onto his lap.

I'm fully straddling him, one leg on either side of his hips, my heat pressing directly over his hard length. "Jack. Tell me. Tell me you don't see me. That I'm nothing but your sick little niece, craving her uncle's heart, body, and soul."

My words are garbled, thick with emotion. I need him to kill this thing inside of me. With each passing second, this need consumes me, growing inch by inch and taking over my soul, leaving nothing but this desire to love and be loved.

Jack's hand move to cup my face, his eyes glistening as they bounce back and forth between mine. "I can't, Princess. I just can't." He brings my face closer to his, our lips hovering over one another. "It'd be a lie. One I only voiced to protect you."

A ragged sob is pulled from my lips, the motion making them brush salty wet tears across Jack's mouth.

His warm tongue swipes at the swollen flesh before replacing it with soft pecks and pulling away. "Pen, I love you. But part of loving you means wanting what's best for you, and that's not always going to be what I want."

I suck in a sharp breath at his words. *He loves me.*

But just as quickly as he gave me wings, he clipped them back down. "I think you should go to college. Live your life like a normal girl your age would."

I blink, not understanding how he could build me up one moment and then shatter me in the next. "Jack, there is nothing normal about me. I'm the farthest thing from it. Can't you see that college isn't for me? Can't you see that what I want is right here, with the kids, with *you*?"

I press my core to him, grinding my swollen nub along his rigid cock, the action ripping a groan from us both.

"Pen," Jack moans out a warning we both know he doesn't mean.

I'm about to roll my hips again when the clattering of metal has me whipping my head around.

Standing at the entrance of Jack's study is Mary, a surprised look washing over her usually happy features. "I'm… Excuse, me sir. I came to collect the mugs. I didn't know anyone was still in here."

Jack's face is red, his hands gripping tightly onto my hips, but making no move to remove me from his lap. "Thank you,

Mary. That won't be necessary. Pen and I will clean up."

The older woman gives us a nod, her gaze never leaving the ground. "Very well. I'll see you both in the morning then."

Without another word, she hightails it out of the office and vanishes into the hall.

Jack loosens his grip on my hips, a shallow breath escaping his parted lips. "That could've been worse."

I smile. "Oh yeah? How's that?"

"Given a few more minutes, she would've caught me shoving my hard cock inside that warm little cunt of yours."

I release a gasp which quickly turns into a squeak as Jack lifts me by the hips and deposits me in front of him, both of us now standing.

With narrowed eyes and a flush face, he begins to pick up the mugs left behind by the kids. "I think she saved us both. Hell, that was probably Austin watching over us, sending her to cock block me from doing something stupid."

He mumbles more to himself, but his words hit me straight in the chest, making me stumble as I pick up my glass.

"Fuck. That's not *what* or *how* I meant it, Pen." He takes a step toward me, but then stops. "You and I both know that this isn't right. Despite how good and right it might feel. You're too young. You have so much life to live, and I'm not going to be the selfish prick who stops you from living it. You'll resent me later."

"For someone who's lived a lot longer than I have, you sure are blind. But that's fine. I won't force myself on you anymore." My heart feels heavy in my chest, the words I'm speaking cracking it wide open. "You said that you loved me, but this isn't love. This is fear, and I don't fuck with cowards."

Not able to hear another word, I storm out of the study and toward the kitchen. This day has been too much. I can't take another second. All I want to do is go up to my room and bury myself under the covers, letting sleep and darkness wash over me.

To hell with today. Tomorrow will be better.

FILTHY CROWN

Chapter Twenty-Three

JACK

I don't fuck with cowards.

Pen's words from last night keep rattling in my head, making my blood pressure spike.

"Who's a coward?" Jace sneaks up behind me, making me spill the coffee I'd just been pouring.

"Jesus. Who taught you to walk around like that? A ninja?"

"Yes. Now don't change the subject." He slaps me on the back, a wicked grin stretching across his lips. "Who's a coward?"

Does he know what happened in the study last night? He couldn't, could he?

"Nobody. Are you ready to ride with the kids this morning? I was thinking we would keep them close to the house until we hear otherwise from security. As it is, we're keeping everyone here. Even moving in Dr. Leventhal and his partner. Just in case."

Jace is nodding when Matt and Hunter walk into the kitchen.

"How's that going, the therapy sessions with the kids?" Hunter asks and Matt cuts in.

"And by kids, he also means Pen." Matt raises a brow as he goes to pull a mug from the cupboard.

I roll my eyes and take a sip of the dark liquid before responding. "As well as could be expected. It's only been a little over two weeks, so there's been little improvement in the nightmare department with Amanda. I have the monitor set up in her room and I've been letting Pen handle that whenever she wakes up. I feel like my presence would be too much for her in a groggy state. The last thing I think she'd need is a looming male figure."

Jace's fists clench over the countertop, his face growing red with anger. "Those fuckers need to pay for what they've done. This can't go unavenged."

My brows practically hit my hairline. "That's a drastic change from not wanting to go near the cartel. Wasn't that your position on this whole expedition?"

Jace scoffs. "That was before I saw the kids. It's real now. Seeing how affected they all are, even Pen."

"Even Pen what?" Penelope walks in with both kids in tow, and I have to make a concerted effort not to go to her and take her in my arms.

I don't fuck with cowards. Her words hit me like a bucket of iced water. I'm no fucking coward and the need to prove her wrong is so strong my feet start carrying me toward her.

As if reading what's on my mind, Hunter steps between us, his palm landing square on my chest as his head shakes back and forth.

"So, is anyone going to answer me or are we all going to stand here in silence?" Pen raises a brow, her eyes bouncing between all of the Crown brothers.

"Someone's in a mood this morning." Jace teases, his gaze falling on me as if I were the reason for the attitude.

He's not wrong, but there's no way in hell I'd ever admit to it. "It's nothing that needs to be discussed right now." I look toward the kids and usher them to the table where Mary has a full spread out for us to enjoy. "Eat up, kids. We're riding in thirty."

Amanda and Alex don't have to be told twice. Within seconds, they're both seated and piling eggs and bacon onto their plates.

Pen, on the other hand, is still standing with both arms crossed over her ample chest.

"Sit, Pen. You'll need food to keep up your energy for the ride." I urge her to sit, but my hands remain at my side for fear that I might reach out and touch her inappropriately.

"Yes, Daddy," Pen mutters as she sits in her chair, her words both temptation and torture wrapped up in one sinful package.

Things I want to do to her flash before me and my dick takes notice, swelling to its full length, ready and eager to meet the challenge.

"Christ, Jack," Matt mutters under his breath, his hand clamping down on my shoulder. "Get a grip, brother."

My eyes meet his and I know he's seen the tent I'm sporting.

Quickly maneuvering myself behind the counter, I try for a change of subject. One I know will be sure to sour the mood. "Dr. Leventhal will be moving into the main house."

Everyone at the table stops what they're doing, their eyes focusing on me. "Now, I know you aren't a fan of therapy, but we think it'll be better for everyone if the doctors could observe us in our everyday life. Get us all back to healed and happy as soon as possible."

Pen narrows her eyes. Her bullshit radar probably going off and calling me out on my partial lie. It's true that I want the doctor to be here for them in case Pen has another attack or another nightmare happens where Pen can't soothe Amanda. But a big reason for their moving in is out of safety.

With the cartel possibly being out here, I don't want to risk our guests being targeted.

"I don't think that's necessary." Pen bristles, it's obvious she doesn't like Leventhal.

"It's only temporary. I think we can all make the sacrifice, just for a little bit."

She's about to open her mouth in what I think is a rebuttal when Sam comes rushing in, his face as pale as snow. "Sir. A word."

I nod, looking toward Pen before I follow him out. "You good with the kids?"

She nods, her eyes never leaving Sam's face. There's trouble, and she knows it.

I make it out of the kitchen and down the hall when I hear boots behind me. Turning, I see all Crown brothers are following. Seems they caught wind of trouble, too.

Entering my office, I instruct Hunter to shut the door. This seems serious and I don't want anyone to overhear.

"Speak up, Sam." I sit on my desk, not bothering with the chair.

"The horses, sir." Sam's face goes from white to green and my stomach drops.

"What's happened to the horses, Sam?"

"They've been gutted." Choked sounds erupt around the room, none of us having expected this.

I'm blinking long hard blinks, my breathing picking up with each intake of breath. "Have you told anyone of this?"

"No, sir. I came straight here. They were all in their stalls. Extremely quiet. Too quiet. I went in to check on them before this morning's ride when I found them. Each and every one, sir." His eyes well up and I know this has to be hard for him. He loved those horses as much as me, if not more.

Walking toward him, I place both hands on his shoulders. "Listen, Sam. This can't get out to the rest of the staff. Take one or two of our most trusted men, clear the area and then send the rest of the crew home. Tell them we'll be shutting down operations and keeping a skeleton crew. At least for a couple of weeks."

He nods in agreement, his face rife with determination. "Yes, sir."

"Good. Once you're done with that, I'll need you to come back here. We have some things to discuss. And Sam, I want you to know that your hard work and dedication to this family isn't going unnoticed. You're like family. I hope you know that you and yours will always be cared for."

Sam nods, his eyes welling up once more before he turns and walks out of the room without another word.

As soon as the door shuts behind him, Jace lets out a low whistle. "Christ. There's no doubt it's those sick fuckers who followed us down here."

"No shit. What are we going to do now? They taunted us with the gas, but this is some next level fuckery."

I rub at the back of my neck. "What's troubling is that they targeted the horses. Did they somehow know we were going to be riding this morning? Are they listening now? We need to get the men of WRATH down here and see if they have a signal jammer or something while we discuss our next moves."

All of them agree, nodding vigorously.

"Okay. I'll message them and we'll start this back up when they get here. In the meantime. Let's get the kids and all their shit packed up as soon as possible. One thing is clear, we're not staying here."

"You can't stay here." Titus's words match up with what I was thinking. "Your property is too large for us to cover and it hasn't been set up with our surveillance. Not like our property back in Texas."

"So what are you saying?" Jace looks toward Titus, but it's Hudson who answers.

"We have a couple of safe homes in Texas. They're fully decked out with surveillance and escape tunnels should we need them. We think y'all should come back with us."

Titus cuts in, "No offense, but we're taking our women and children from the ranch. As beautiful as it is up here, now is not the time to be enjoying nature. Not with whoever's running amuck."

"No offense taken. I was just telling the guys that we need to be packing up the kids. This property was built for leisure, not high-level defense. Although, that'll be changing soon. I'll never be caught off guard like this again."

Hudson speaks up, "We can help you get that all set up once we've got the current threat neutralized. In the meantime, get everyone packed up and we'll be shipping out within the hour."

I nod. "Thank you, again. We appreciate everything you've done for our family."

"I said it once and I'll say it again. It's what we do. Unfortunately, we have to be at your service once more, but hopefully sometime soon our visits will be all pleasure and no business. The kids love it here, and at the rate we're going, there'll be a full brood of WRATH kids storming the mountains every summer."

A broad smile spreads across my face. "Now that's something to look forward to."

Clapping him on the back, I walk the men to the door, signaling for my brothers to follow.

"Better get to it then." Hunter passes by me in the hall, heading toward the kitchen where the kids have been hanging out, patiently waiting for a ride that will never come. "I'll be the bad guy and tell them horseback riding has been tabled."

I'd give him a nod of gratitude, but his back is to me, his feet carrying him swiftly toward the kitchen.

"No need to walk us out." Hudson waves a hand. "You have packing to do yourself. Titus will stay here and watch guard, the rest of us will be here within the hour to escort you to the airfield."

With another clap to the shoulder, Hudson walks off, leaving us to get ready to head to god knows where. All I know is that anywhere is safer than the ranch, where wide open spaces leave us exposed like sitting ducks.

Wasting no time, I head toward the study where my firearms are stored. They're coming with us. Come hell or high water, I swear no harm will come to those kids. They've been through enough and if I have to lay down my life to keep them safe, then so be it.

They're worth that and more.

FILTHY CROWN

Chapter Twenty-Four

PENELOPE

"**D**id you bring everything you needed?" Ashley asks from the front passenger seat. We're in a blacked out Suburban and this is giving me all sorts of déjà vu.

But instead of her and Titus taking us to Jack's home in Colorado, now we're all leaving and headed to a safe house somewhere outside of Dallas, Texas.

I've never been before, but the weather seems mild and the scenery is a hell of a lot more city than the ranch.

Finally pulling my vision from the vanishing skyline, I look toward Ashley. "I have everything except for my hairbrush. I couldn't find it anywhere."

"Did you misplace it?" Jack cuts into our conversation, his broad shoulder bumping into me as he speaks, the small contact sending a shiver up my spine.

Stop it. I scold my treacherous body. I'm still mad at him for pushing me away and thinking he knows what's best for me.

"No. I don't think so. I've always left it in the same place, but I can't be too sure with how crazy things have been lately." I'm chewing on my bottom lip, wondering where I could've left it when Jack reaches out and plucks the tender flesh between his fingers.

"Don't do that, Pen." He closes his eyes before releasing his hold and turning toward the front of the vehicle. "Ashley, is there somewhere we can stop for a hairbrush or is this something you carry at the safe house."

Ashley smirks, her eyes dancing between Jack and me. "We have brushes at the house, but I'd be happy to accommodate any special requests. I know I'm particular about what I use on my hair. Just let me know, Pen, and I'll hook you up."

"Thank you." I let out a sigh. I'm not looking forward to this new form of captivity. It may not be as bad as the cartel, but the kids and I are still being held against our will, unable to leave the property. That's definitely going to mess with our heads. "Maybe you and the girls can pop over if things get too boring and we can have a girls' night."

Titus bristles at my words, and Ashley doesn't miss it. Placing her hand on his bicep, she tries to smooth over the request. "That sounds like fun. I'm sure our big strong men can make something happen. After all, what good is having a security team for a family if they can't even accommodate a couple of girlfriends hanging out."

Oh, she's good. Complimenting him to where his refusal

would be seen as his inability to protect us seems to do the trick.

Titus gives her side eye, but the smirk on his lips tells me he knows full well what she's doing. Even so, he doesn't dispute her, signaling that he's already softening to the idea.

Thank god, because I don't know how I'm going to handle being locked up in close quarters with Jack. Not after everything that's happened this past week.

I meant what I said. I'm not going to keep throwing myself at him. I've already done it way too much and with his track history of leaving me hanging, I'm not willing to risk my heart anymore.

I turn toward the back of the SUV and see that the kids are asleep. I don't blame them; we've been driving for what feels like ages.

"How much longer?" I whisper into the cab.

"We're here," Titus announces, his booming voice making the kids stir.

I turn to look out the window and see we're pulling into a gated neighborhood, the main road taking us down a winding path to a cute little farmhouse settled amongst a thicket of trees.

My eyes narrow on the modest structure. "How many rooms are there?" I'm trying to gauge by the size, and it's not looking very promising. Especially not if Mary will be staying with us.

"Four bedrooms and a study," Jack speaks up. "You'll take the master. The kids will each have their own room. And Mary will be just down the hall if you need help with anything."

My brows push together, wondering where it leaves him. "And you? Where will you and your brothers stay?"

"He'll be sleeping in the study. As for Jace, Hunter, and Matt, they'll be in the house caddy corner to this one with Dr. Leventhal, his associate and Georgina." Ashley raises a brow, giving me a mischievous smile.

"Georgina? But I thought you fired her." I shoot Jack an accusatory glare, wondering why this tramp is still around.

His eyes bore into mine. "She's no longer my employee, but I couldn't throw her on her ass and leave her to fend for herself with all that we have going on right now. What if they've made her a target because of her connection? Would you really be okay with something happening to her because of us?"

His words hit deep, and even though I know they make sense, I can't get my jealous heart to calm the fuck down.

Blowing out a frustrated breath, I change the topic back to our living situation and choose to ignore Georgina and her skank-ass ways all together.

"Well, you don't have to sleep in the study. I can just share a room with Amanda." I'm staring straight at him, asking him to make sense of this. Who'd want to sleep in a study instead of an actual bedroom if they don't have to?

"Dr. Leventhal thinks it'd be best if Amanda kept some semblance of routine. She's always had her own room so this move shouldn't make her sleeping situation any different. He thinks it could make her night terrors worse."

I cross my arms and pout. That's the most ridiculous thing I've ever heard. If anything, I think it would comfort her, having her big sister close by. "I think you need to question whoever said Dr. Leventhal was the best. Maybe get a second opinion, because some of his suggestions seem illogical."

"I'll do that, Princess." Jack smirks, making my heart rate

spike and blood boil all at once.

"Wanting a second opinion isn't amusing, Jack." I'm glaring at him when the door to the SUV opens. Turning to look, I see one of the security detail is standing guard. "Is all this really necessary? Having someone walk us to a door?"

I'm in denial. If the cartel is still after us, then yes, of course this is necessary. But my mind doesn't want to accept it. I finally got a taste of freedom after a week of hell, and I'm just not ready to give it up.

I'm about to step out into the drive when Jack's strong hands pull me back into his chest, his lips hovering over the shell of my ear. "Listen here, Princess. When I say something, it isn't a suggestion. You'll obey me or so help me god, my spanking you raw will be the least of your worries."

A shiver wracks through me, his words turning me on. Instantly, heat pools at my core and my pussy clenches. God, why does he have to be so infuriating and sexy all at the same time?

Jerking myself free, I don't even bother looking back. Instead, I look toward the rear, pulling Amanda free from her car seat and into my arms.

My panties may be soaked and I might be pulsing with need, but Hell will freeze over before I ever show that man he affects me.

Jack

I swear that girl is trying my patience.

Gritting my teeth, I watch Pen and her detail disappear into the house with both kids still knocked out from the trip.

I'm still staring at the closed door when Titus comes up beside me, his open palm slapping me on the back. "I wish I could tell you it gets easier, brother. But it doesn't."

"What doesn't?" I turn to look at him and see that the corner of his mouth is tilted up in a smirk.

"You know what I'm talking about. Especially now that you'll be on lockdown together. But hey, look on the bright side…"

"There's a bright side to this?" I raise a brow incredulously.

"Yes." Titus leans in, his words whispered for my ears only. "Texas doesn't have a Romeo and Juliet law, so there's nothing stopping you if it's consensual."

His words wash over me as the realization that Pen is now fair game hits me square in the chest.

My heart pounds as my mind reels. Visions of my fat cock thrusting in and out of Pen's little cunt flash before me, the sinful thoughts making me swell to the point of pain.

What kind of filthy fuck am I? Here we are, in a safe house, and all I'm thinking about is ramming my cock into Pen's tight little pussy.

Shaking my head, I try to rid myself of these images. I need to do a better job of keeping things straight. I'm her guardian, not her lover.

"Thanks for the info, brother. But I'm still her uncle."

Titus raises a brow, his smirk never leaving his lips. "You and I both know that's legally inaccurate."

"Even so, Pen has attached a familial relationship to Jack."

Dr. Leventhal speaks up behind us and my skin prickles, wondering just how much he'd heard. "I think Jack is the best option for a guardian, seeing as how he's the eldest and can provide some sort of structure for her before she's off to college."

Maybe he *didn't* hear everything. A man can only hope. "Yes. She'll be staying at the safe house with me. Thank you again for your help with the kids. I understand these aren't normal circumstances, but I want you to know that my brothers and I appreciate you working around our particular situation."

"No need to thank me, Jack. You're already paying me more than enough to compensate for any discomfort the living arrangements may cause. If it's okay with you, I'd like to come over tonight and check in with the kids. Make sure they're settling into their new environment."

"Actually, I'd prefer it if you came in the morning." I look back toward the house and wonder if the kids are still asleep. "Today has already been trying enough, and I want to make sure they're settled in before we start poking at any feelings. Just give them some room to breathe, yeah?"

Dr. Leventhal gives me a tight smile, clearly unhappy with my demand, but I couldn't care less. Those kids deserve at least one night of normalcy, or as close as we can get to it with everything going on. "Very well then, I'll see you all tomorrow morning."

Titus speaks up, reminding us of his presence. "I'll have one of our men walk you over." He's speaking into his radio when someone emerges from a neighboring home. "Our team is occupying the entire street. Should either of you need to leave the premises at any point, there'll be someone at your disposal. We just ask that you don't exit your homes without first alerting a team member." Titus motions toward the man who's dressed in civilian clothing. "Doctor, whenever you're ready."

Dr. Leventhal nods, following the guard and disappearing into his temporary home.

Reaching a hand toward Titus, I try to convey my gratitude for what feels like the millionth time. "I don't think I could ever say it enough, but thank you."

"No need, Jack. It's what we do. Besides, you'll be hosting the team every summer, so I'd say it's more than a fair trade."

I chuckle. "It's nowhere near the same, but I'll take it."

Titus's smirk returns. "Now how about you stop wasting time out here and go face the music. Doesn't seem like your little lady is too happy with you right now."

I give his shoulder a shove. "If I didn't know any better, I'd say you were rooting for our sick little relationship."

Titus outright snorts. "Brother, if that makes you sick, then all the men of WRATH belong in a mental ward. Trust me, you guys aren't anything special, so stop torturing yourself over it."

I'm shaking my head as I walk into the house, wondering if his words hold any water. Now that laws aren't an obstacle, what's holding me back from taking what I want?

Nothing. Absolutely nothing.

FILTHY CROWN

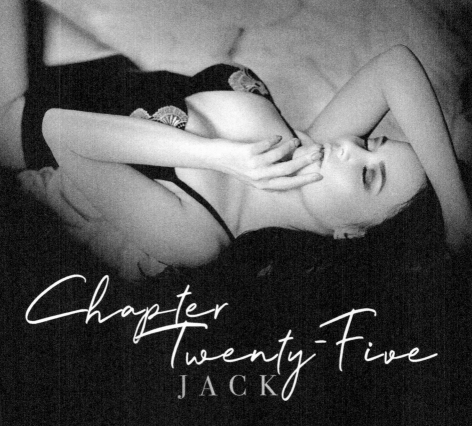

Chapter Twenty-Five

JACK

We've spent the rest of the day together as a family. Currently, the kids are splayed out in front of the television while Pen and I take the couch.

A cartoon animation is playing on the big screen, something about a kid who lives underwater and wants to see the outside world. I want to tell him it's overrated and the safety of the water is so much better, but that's insane. This is a movie. The kid isn't real.

It's clear my current situation is affecting me more than I care to lead on.

"You okay?" Pen whispers, scooting closer to me.

Lifting my arm, I extend it along the back of the couch and behind Pen. "Yes, just a lot on my mind."

She nods, a small yawn playing on her gorgeous mouth. With the hand that's directly behind her, I pull her head to my shoulder. "Rest, Princess. It's been a long day."

Despite her attitude earlier, she complies. Lowering my lips to the top of her head, I whisper an apology. "I'm sorry."

She looks up at me, her big honey-colored eyes widening. "Why? I mean, there's so much to be sorry for."

Her lip curls up in a smirk, and I can't help but take my free hand and tickle her ribs. She squeals but tries to muffle it, glancing over at the kids to make sure they haven't heard.

"Smartass." I raise a brow, the wide grin on my face letting her know it's a playful dig. "I'm sorry for everything you're having to go through now. I promise it won't always be like this."

She nods. Her face turning solemn. No more words are said as she lays her head back down and focuses on the movie.

It doesn't take long for her to fully pass out. Wanting her to get some much needed rest, I place a pillow on my lap and lay her head down, extending her legs so she's fully laid out. We're about half way through the movie and I know she'll get a wicked cramp if she stays in an awkward angle.

Taking a moment of selfish pleasure, I let my eyes roam her body. Soaking in the curve of her hip, the swell of her breast, her beautiful hair. She's so fucking gorgeous it takes everything in me to keep my hands to myself.

Earlier, I'd mistakenly thought there was nothing stopping me from taking what I wanted. What I needed.

But that was selfish. What about what Pen needs? She's so damn young. She still has so much life to live. I'd be a fucking monster if I inserted myself, demanding her love and affection.

There's no doubt that if I let myself have Pen, I'd want all of her, taking everything she had until there was nothing left but me and her. I'd consume every bit of joy and pleasure she could give, only stopping when I've taken my last breath.

Pen stirs in her sleep, her hands pushing off the pillow beneath her head and leaving it directly on my lap. To be precise, her cheek is resting directly on my cock.

Fuck. It twitches, the length pushing up against her face, making me swallow back a groan.

God, this isn't good. I'm about to move her when she starts rubbing her little face in my lap, her partially open mouth absently stroking up and down my length, making my cock painfully harder.

Christ. Visions of Pen taking my dick in her mouth makes the fucker jump up and press against her cheek again, the motion making Pen startle. She turns, so she's now fully on her back, her face looking up at me with wide eyes.

I give her a sheepish smile and whisper, "Sorry. He can't help it."

Her brow raises. "And you? Can you help it?"

I let out a slow breath and shake my head no. No matter how hard I try or what I tell myself is right and fair, I can't help but want her.

Pen reaches for the throw blanket on the back of the couch and throws it over herself. As soon as her body is covered, she takes my hand and brings it to her exposed stomach. "Prove it. Show me you can't help it."

A current of energy zaps between us and I gladly let her skin burn me, accepting the fact that I'm going straight to hell. She's everything I need, everything I want, and I'll willingly go up in flames for just a taste.

My open palm travels up her bare stomach, only stopping when my fingers touch the soft underside of her breast.

I suck in a sharp breath when I realize she isn't wearing a bra, her young supple tits free for me to grope. Pen's breathing hitches as my hand moves higher, my palm rubbing against her pebbled nipple back and forth.

She lets out a tiny mewl and my dick pulses, wanting inside her. The movement makes her lips curl up into a wicked smirk, one of her hands raising up behind her head so she can stroke me.

I groan as soon as her slender fingers wrap around my jersey clad cock. Not letting her have all the fun, I take her hard little nipple and pinch it between my thumb and forefinger, her eyes rolling back in sync with the movement.

Removing my hand, I bring a finger to her mouth and whisper, "Suck."

She takes me into her mouth, swirling the digit around her tongue, her eyes never leaving mine.

"*Fuck, baby.*" I slowly pull my finger free, glancing up to make sure the movie is still playing and the kids are occupied.

Once satisfied, I lower my hand back under the covers and return to her perky tits, spreading her moisture on the pebbled flesh. What I'd give for it to be my mouth instead of my fingers, flicking the hard little nubs with my tongue.

"*Mine.*" My fingers grope her tit to the point of bruising, making Pen choke back a squeal.

This need to have her is all-consuming. The realization that this isn't a passing craze is made all the more real when a violent urge hits me. I need to take her. Have my way with her.

I've desperately tried to stay away, but there's not much more I can take.

My hands roam her slender body, seeking salvation, freedom from this wicked urge that's possessed every cell of my being. The only answer, the only way out, is through. I need to have her. Maybe then this monster will be sated.

My hand drops lower and lower, seeking the only thing that'll feed the beast. It won't stop until her body is one with mine, melded to the point of unity.

Pen's body shakes in anticipation as my fingers dip below her waistband, her silent whimpers registering somewhere in the background of this fog I'm in, but I'm too forgone to stop.

A thick digit slides between her slick folds, her pussy bare and primed, ready for licking. *Take. Take. Take.* The beast calls. Unable to ignore its demands, I press hard against her little pearl, her thighs squeezing my hand with a grip I can't wait to feel against my hips.

Needing more, I slide two fingers inside her channel, the tightness of her walls constricting against their girth.

Pen tenses, her eyes open wide and mouth hanging open. "Oh. God." She blinks up at me in wonder.

A small smirk plays on my lips. What I could show this girl… I'd give her the world if she'd let me. Taking my thumb, I stroke her clit, making her buck into my hand.

"You'll have to stay still if you want to play, Princess." I stroke her hair with my free hand, all while I continue working her tight pussy.

She's so wet for me, she's making tiny squelching noises as I pump in and out of her, the sound making my mouth beg for a taste.

"Open, baby." I growl while pushing at her inner thigh with my pinky.

"Yes, Daddy," Pen whispers, and my head immediately flings back, pressing against the couch. *She's killing me.*

Punishing her, I pump harder, fucking her hard with my fingers, wishing it were my cock instead. She mewls and my free hand flies to her mouth. I shake my head no while I continue my rough strokes, curving the pads of my fingers so I'm hitting that secret spot inside her.

She closes her eyes, her mouth opening and her teeth sinking into my flesh, the sting of her bite making this so much hotter.

"That's right, baby. Take it," I whisper through clenched teeth.

She's close. I can feel her pulsing around my fingers. Giving her that final push, I take my thumb and press it to her clit.

In that moment, I swear I see heaven in her eyes. She's opened them wide, her mouth going slack.

My fingers slow, stretching out her pleasure and drawing out every twitch, every spasm her body has to offer. I take it all because it's mine. It all belongs to me. She belongs to me.

As her body softens in my hold, I know. There is no other woman for me. I'll wait all eternity if I have to, but this is it. She's the one.

I'm sick. I'm a sick old man, pacing back and forth in front of his niece's bedroom.

The entire time we were running through the bedtime routine with the kids, I couldn't stop thinking about Pen and how her tiny frame writhed beneath me. Like a fiend who's had a taste, I want more. I want it all.

I keep telling myself that it'll be just this time. That I'll let her go after I've been sated. I'll let her live her life, go off to college and fall in love with some stupid prick I'll no doubt hate.

My fists clench at the thought, my chest vibrating with rage at the vision of her with some other man. A man who isn't me.

Pressing my head to the door, I let the coolness of the wood clear my head. This is wrong. What I did was wrong. She's young and impressionable. She doesn't know what she wants.

I'm about to turn around and head back to the study when her door swings open, a startled look painted on her face.

"Jack." Her lips are parted, her little tongue poking out and licking at the rosy flesh.

Like a bull seeing a red flag, I charge. My hands go to her rib cage, the fingers gripping around her tightly while I push her back into the room, my lips finding hers and issuing a punishing kiss where I devour her whole.

Fuck right or wrong. I need her. *Right. Now.*

"Pen, baby. Tell me you don't want this before I've lost all control." I manage to pry my lips from her enough to look back at her eyes, mine bouncing back and forth between her dark honey orbs.

In the dim light of the room I can see her pupils are blown

out, and I only pray it's because she wants this too.

"Oh, Jack." Her fingers grip onto my shirt, pushing the material up and off. "It's about fucking time."

Her sass, even now, pulls a low chuckle from my lips, but it quickly dies when she drops to her knees and her slender hands fall to my waist.

Big doe eyes look up at me as she licks her lips, she's waiting as if asking permission, wanting me to take control. *My fucking pleasure.*

"Take it out and suck," I growl through clenched teeth, my dick threatening to rip out of my sleep pants.

With no more prompting, my little princess does as she's told. Her small hand finds me and sets me free in more ways than one.

My eyes never leave her sensual mouth as her pink pouty lips slip over the crown, taking me into her warmth and making me let out a feral noise that comes from deep within. This is where I belong, inside my baby.

I throw my head back and roar, my eyes rolling back as she swirls her tongue around me, one of her hands gripping and gently squeezing my balls.

Fuck. I'm lost. Lost to this woman for as long as she'll have me.

I'd walk through broken glass and swim through the flames of hell if it meant I could have her. *She's mine, and I'm not giving her up.*

FILTHY CROWN

Chapter
Twenty-Six
PENELOPE

He's big and thick, making my mind race, wondering how he'll feel inside me, stretching me and filling me up.

A whimper escapes me as I take him in, his velvety shaft sliding in and out of my mouth, bumping the back of my throat and making me swallow.

"Fuck, Princess. You know how much Daddy loves that."

Hell. Yes, I do. I love this. Bringing out the dirty side of Jack.

Already slick with need, his filthy words have my pussy clenching. Wanting to push him, I hum around his length, the vibrations making him buck into me and making me gag.

That's right, Daddy. Give me that big cock.

Moaning, I pull back, sucking on the mushroom tip, reveling in the musky taste of his precum. I'm mid swirl when his hand comes to the back of my head, his fingers gripping tightly onto my hair and pulling me off.

"No more, Princess. I need inside that pretty pussy." Jack lowers himself, his hands coming to my shoulders, roughly pushing me down onto the cold floor before traveling to my breasts. "God, you're so fucking perfect. Too perfect for me."

"No. I was made for you, Jack." My hand reaches up, the fingers tracing the moonlit contours of his rugged face. He's the perfect one, with his high cheekbones and strong jaw, it's a miracle he isn't already taken.

He's mine. That's why. A voice in the recesses of my brain screams. Yes. I was made for him and he was made for me.

Jack has pushed up my nightgown, his hands now resting on my rib cage, fingers digging into me possessively as his gaze travels up and down my frame.

"Like what you see, Daddy?"

"Fuck, you're so damn beautiful." His lips come down to a silk-covered nipple, his teeth plucking at it, sucking in the peak through the fabric.

My back arches off the ground, pressing my breast further into him as a moan escapes me. "Take me, please. I can't take it anymore."

I told myself I wasn't going to beg. That I wasn't going to throw myself at him anymore, but fuck it. All sense of self-preservation flew out the window as soon as his lips landed on mine.

"But I thought I was a coward. Isn't that what you said?" Jack's mouth curls up into a smirk as he travels to my other breast, giving it the same attention as he sucks at it through the fabric. "Cowards don't fuck their little girls, do they?"

His fingers travel up to the strap of my nightgown, his movements painfully slow as I narrow my eyes at him. "Jack," I growl, my hips moving, grinding my core on his stomach as my legs wrap around him and lock him into place. "A coward doesn't finger fuck his little girl with other people in the room."

I raise a brow, begging him to argue. Come hell or high water, he isn't leaving until he's had me. Not until I've felt his massive length inside of me.

Reminding him of what I want, of what's his to take, I lower my hand, gripping his thick shaft. Using the head of his cock, I push the thin fabric of my panties to the side and drag the turgid tip along my slick folds, letting him feel the heat, feel how wet he's made me.

"Don't you want me, Daddy? Don't you want to make me feel good?" I whisper, my eyes never leaving his, knowing our little game affects him as much as it does me.

He closes his eyes, fighting my hold, but I don't give up. Taking him in hand, I give him one hard stroke before I push the tip into my channel.

The one little movement makes my back arch and legs quiver. *God, he feels so good.*

"*Fuck*, Princess." He retreats before shallowly pumping the tip back in, not moving any further, his restraint driving me crazy with need. "You know this is wrong, right? You know once we cross this line, we can't take it back?"

I whimper, the fog of lust and love so strong I can barely form words. My hands scrape down his chest and then wrap around his back, bringing his chest down onto mine and making him slide in a little bit deeper.

Gasping into his ear, I give him permission. "I'm yours. Always have been. Always will be."

He releases a pained sound, his lips finding the crook of my neck and sucking hard as he thrusts the rest of the way in, taking me to the hilt and breaking through whatever's left of my barrier in one swift move.

A whimper of pain falls from my lips, making Jack still. He releases his hold on my neck, his eyes finding mine as a lone tear escapes down my face.

"I should apologize, but I won't." He lowers his face, his tongue lapping up at the rogue tear before he slowly pulls his length out, only to thrust it back in. "This is mine, Pen. Your perfect little cunt is mine and there isn't a man on this earth who'd dare say otherwise."

His movements are slow and rough, his possessiveness making the pain melt away, replacing it with burning heat.

I breathe out, shaky and slow, our eyes dancing in the moonlight. "I'm all yours and you're all mine."

"I'm yours, baby." His open palm finds my heart, splaying his fingers wide before he drives into me so hard my body slides up the hardwood floor. "Every fucking bit of me is yours until the day I die."

His words bring me to tears. I'm unable to stop the flow as, one after another, they fall down my face.

I didn't know how much I'd long to hear them until this very moment. He's mine. I have him. *My big strong Jack.*

He lowers his chest to mine, his lips placing frantic kisses all over my face while he continues to slide in and out of me.

"Don't cry, Princess. Daddy's got you and he's never letting you go."

Oh, my-fucking-god. If I thought his words before wrecked me, he's now decimated me. He's ripped me wide open and stitched me back together. Giving me what I've needed all these years.

This game we play, it might be sick to some, but it's what my soul needs. This broken little girl inside me needed love, needed safety, needed her daddy to make her whole. Jack knows that. He sees it. Sees me. And instead of judging me, he gives it to me. Holds me together and makes me complete.

A ragged sob is ripped from me as I pull him to me, my arms gripping onto him for dear life. "I love you. God, I love you so fucking much."

I buck into him with all that I have, needing to feel him tearing me in two because I know... I know with every fiber of my being that he's the only one who can put me back together.

Jack lets out a feral growl as his hands find my ass, his fingers gripping into the meaty flesh. His thrusts turn punishing as he drives his hard length in and out of me.

Hard. Brutal. Thrusts.

My body bouncing and sliding up the floor, only held in place by his grip on my ass. "Yes, take me. Make me yours, Daddy."

"Always," he grits out, his eyes finding where we're connected. "Jesus, Princess. Your cunt looks so good wrapped around my cock." He slows his thrusts, they're now coming excruciatingly slow. "God, baby. You were made for me. Made for Daddy."

Just when I think I'm about to explode from his words, his

hand leaves its hold on my backside and travels around to my mound. As soon as his finger presses on my bundle of nerves, I explode.

A kaleidoscope of colors floods my vision as a sound I don't recognize is ripped from my throat.

Holymotherfuckingshit. The room tilts and I can't see anything but an explosion of colors as wave after wave of pleasure courses through me.

This is it. He's it. The missing piece to my jagged puzzle, making me whole.

He said there's no going back, and I don't want to. I'm finally where I need to be. Happy and whole.

"So." *Thrust.* "Damn." *Thrust.* "Beautiful."

Jack keeps thrusting into me, his movements now coming fast and jerky.

"Squeeze, baby. Make your daddy cum." Jack grabs my hand and brings it to his family jewels, pressing my fingers into him.

I do as he says, my walls clenching around him as my fingers hold him tight. "Gaaaaarrrhhhhhh," Jack roars into the room, his body stilling save for the jerking of his cock deep inside me, each twitch releasing a spurt of warmth and coating me with his love.

He stays inside me, keeping us connected even after he's given me every drop. With his arms under mine, he grabs hold and lifts us both off the floor, my body soft and compliant now that it's been thoroughly fucked.

Reaching my bed, he finally pulls out—our joint liquid trailing down my partially covered pussy, our cum soaking my panties and leaking onto my thigh. Others might find this gross, but I love it. It's a reminder that this was all real. Jack made me his. I'm his.

Pulling me under the covers, his hand roams to my sticky mound. "*Mine.*"

Lowering his head, he places gentle kisses on both peaks before traveling down my stomach and bypassing my scrunched up nightgown to my lace covered pussy.

It's then that it hits me. He took me while partially clothed, not even bothering to fully undress me.

Looking down, I see that he's pulled the soaked fabric to the side, exposing me as his eyes burn into mine. Jack's tongue slowly lathes up my slit before his lips encircle my clit and suck. "Mine. This pussy is mine."

"Yours, Jack. It's yours." I pant, enjoying how his mouth on my sensitive flesh makes my body spark and tingle.

Pleased with my answer, he smiles, returning to my lips and placing a soft kiss before positioning himself behind me and pulling me back into his chest. "Rest Princess, we have a lot to talk about tomorrow."

My stomach flips at his words, not liking the tone he's just taken. Whatever it is, I'll make sure he doesn't back out. Doesn't take back everything that's happened.

This was everything and more, and hell will freeze over before I'll let him take it from me.

Chapter Twenty-Seven
JACK

I fucked up. I promised her I'd always be there for her, and in some form or fashion I know I always will be. But as reality sets in, I know what I have to do, and that's set her free. Let her live her life.

If she comes back to me, then I'll be the luckiest fucker alive. But if she doesn't, then I only have myself to blame.

I let the hot water spray down my back as I press my head into the cool tile, wondering how in the world I'm going to break the news to Pen.

A draft of cold air hits me as the glass door to the shower opens and I know I've run out of time.

Unable to face her, I keep myself facing the wall. "Pen. We can't do this anymore. We have to stop."

Her small hands that had been wrapping around my waist

freeze in place. "Don't do this." Her voice comes out choked, making me turn around so I can hold her in my arms and soothe some of the pain I'm about to cause.

"I'm sorry, Princess, but this is for your own good. You might not see it now, but you'll thank me one day."

She rears her head back and scoffs. "Then you apparently don't know what's good for me. If you knew that, then you'd know that my place is here, with you." Her soft hands delve lower, her expert fingers stroking me just the way I like and making me instantly hard.

"Penelope. No." Despite my protest, I do nothing to stop her. What can I say? I'm a weak fuck.

"Yes, Jack. You know you love watching your dirty little girl, taking you deep, making you come undone." She drops to her knees and, without preamble, takes me into her mouth.

She isn't wrong. I'd love nothing more than to make her filthy, make her swallow my fat cock until she's taking all my cum. "My filthy-filthy Princess. You do love Daddy's cock, don't you?"

She bobs her head up and down, answering me without letting me slip out. Taking me to the back of her throat, she presses my swollen head against the tight hole, playing with my balls while she swallows.

"*Fuuuuck*, baby." I release a string of curse words, enjoying the feeling of her throat choking my cock. The haze of lust lifts slightly as she releases her grip and pulls me out into her mouth. The small reprieve clearing my head enough to give me some sort of sense. "Princess, this is the last time. No more."

She releases me with a pop, standing to her full five-foot-two. "Naughty Daddy." She walks over to the bench seat, sitting down and opening her legs wide, exposing her beautiful pink folds to me. Running a finger up her drenched slit, she hits me with her words. "If you're going to taste your little girl one last time, then you need to fuck me with your tongue before taking me with your cock."

Jesus fucking christ. She's a tsunami, taking me under and washing away any hesitation I'd been hanging onto. Stepping closer, the vision before me makes my cock jump and my tongue beg for a taste.

Pen smiles wide, though it doesn't reach her eyes. They're glassy and, despite her bravado, I know she's feeling the pain of what's to come.

I lower myself between her legs, my hands stroking up her supple thighs. "Beautiful, baby. So fucking beautiful."

"Hurry, Daddy. It hurts. Make it go away." Pen's eyes well up and her bottom lip trembles, her words coming out choked. "Make it all better."

Her voice cracks, pulling me into action, needing to soothe her the only way I know how.

Placing open-mouthed kisses up her thigh, I commit her taste to memory, enjoying my journey to her slick core.

My tongue laps up her juices, enjoying how wet I make her. This is mine. She's this soaked for me, and I won't let a drop go to waste.

Taking one of her legs, I throw it over my shoulder and feast; the whimpers coming from her like sweet honey to a bee. Pure gold.

She's everything to me. No other will ever compare. As I

swirl and flick my tongue on her clit, I know there will be no one else for me.

Pen runs her fingers through my hair, pressing me harder to her lips. "Yes. Just like that, Daddy. Make me feel good."

My filthy girl. A selfish part of me wants to think that I'm the only one who can satisfy her. Give her exactly what she needs. But that's crazy.

As soon as she leaves me, I know there'll be a line of men vying for her affection. The thought makes my blood boil and I take it out on her pussy, sucking without mercy, plunging three fingers into her tight channel and taking no prisoner.

"Shit," Pen hisses, arching her perfect tits into the air as one hand leaves my head and plays with a pert nipple. "More, I need more. I need you."

She pushes me away, her hands frantically reaching for my cock.

Knowing exactly what she wants, I take her tiny waist and lift her into the air, only lowering her body to impale her sopping pussy on my cock.

We both groan as soon as she's sheathed me. *Home.* That's what she is, and we both know it.

Our eyes connect and something crosses between us, an acknowledgment of belonging. She's mine and I'm hers.

"Please." She writhes against me, her tears mixing with the water coming from above. "I need you."

Her choked sob is my kryptonite, driving my hips forward and taking no mercy. I fuck her hard against the shower wall, my drives sliding her up against the tile over and over again until her sobs of pain have turned into ones of pleasure.

I'm breaking us both. With each thrust, each drive into her tight heat, I know I'm breaking us. But it's what she needs. She deserves more than this. More than an older man who's lived so much more life than her.

Pen's nails dig into my shoulder as she bites my neck, her groan mixed with the clenching of her walls around my girth signaling her release. She's coming on my cock and I know I'll never feel anything this good again.

Letting myself go one last time, I continue to pump into her, gripping her ass hard and holding her still only once I've started shooting into her. Rope after rope, my cum coats her walls, willing for it to mark her. Embed into her soul like she has mine.

Cursing out the last of my release, I send out a selfish prayer to the powers that be. I pray to whoever is listening that my little princess returns. That she finds her way back to her home. To a man who promises to be worthy of her.

Pressing one last kiss to her swollen lips, I let her small body slide down, the evidence of our love leaking from her and making my cock twitch one final time before her words cut me down.

"So that's it? You're just letting me go?" Her tear-filled eyes look up at me, begging me to change my mind. But I won't.

"It's what's best, Pen." I go to touch her face but she steps back, leaving my hand hanging mid air.

"Don't. Don't touch me." She steps out of the shower, holding the door open before turning back. "You're a fucking liar. You promised me you wouldn't let go, and yet, here we are. Looks like you're the fucking coward I thought you were."

She closes the door behind her and I know I can't let her go like this. I need to smooth things over. Or at least try.

Stepping out, I pull on a towel and walk after her, seeing she's already in the bedroom, about to pull the door open. "Pen, wait."

"No, Jack. You've said enough." Clad in just a towel, she swings the door open, coming face to face with Dr. Leventhal and two police officers.

What the fuck?

I step closer, pulling the door open and demanding answers. "What is this?"

"I could ask the same." Dr. Leventhal looks at Pen and me, noting our lack of clothing. *Fuck.* "Georgina informed me last night of your inappropriate behavior with your niece. To say that I'm appalled is an understatement. But that's neither here nor there. What's truly disgusting is what I heard when I came to question you about it last night. Your *sounds* could be heard from outside."

I open my mouth to speak when Dr. Leventhal shoves a piece of paper in my hand. '*Emergency Order*' is written in big bold letters. "What the fuck is this?"

I look up and see Titus with a pained expression on his face. In a flash, the officers are escorting Pen out of the room and that's when I hear the kids screaming their lungs out somewhere outside.

Titus speaks, but all I can see is red. "They have an order and are placing the kids in temporary housing until they can determine whether or not they can stay with one of your brothers."

Halfway through his words, I jump into action, tearing into

the officers and demanding that they leave Pen and the kids.

Titus and Hudson come to my side, pulling me off of the policemen. "Jack, stop. You're making this worse. We have our men on it. One of our attorneys is on their way to the courthouse, trying to get a meeting in chambers. You did nothing wrong. We'll get them back."

My body is vibrating with rage as Pen shouts my name, calling for me to keep her safe. The red haze turns black, and all I feel is violence coursing through me. Whoever was a part of this is going to pay. I won't rest until I feel their life slip from my hands.

They messed with the wrong Crown brother and I swear to all that I hold dear, there will be hell to pay.

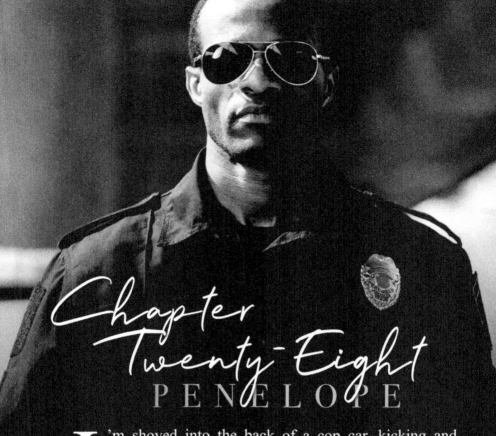

Chapter Twenty-Eight

PENELOPE

I'm shoved into the back of a cop car, kicking and screaming. My cries are made worse when I realize they're placing Amanda and Alex in a separate car. "Stop! I need to be with them. They need me."

My pleas fall on deaf ears as the door shuts and the officers take their position in the front seat, neither bothering to acknowledge me beyond the fact that I'm now their prisoner.

Looking out the window, I see Dr. Leventhal talking to the officers driving the other car and I see him hand them a white envelope. I strain my neck but it's impossible to hear what he's saying.

Needing answers, I bang on the plexiglass partition. "Where are they going? Where are you taking them?"

Nothing. All I get is silence as we pull out of the driveway.

and into the road. A sick feeling settles in my stomach and I know that something isn't right.

Banging on the glass again, I demand their attention. "Hey! Where's my social worker? I want to talk to her. I need to talk to her."

Again. Nothing.

Yeah. Something's definitely not right.

Moving my attention to neighbors or anyone passing by, I bang on the windows. "Help! Help! I've been kidnapped! Help me!"

That seems to do the trick and one of the officers rushes to shove open the partition, but unfortunately for me, he's pointing a gun straight at me.

"*What the fuck?*" I whisper, trying to make sense of what's happening.

Before I can question him again, the trigger goes off and I feel a sting to the neck. The barrel of his gun is the last thing I see before the world goes black and all consciousness leaves me.

Jack

"What do you mean the judge didn't sign the order?" My chest is rising and falling, as blind rage threatens to take hold once more.

Looking around the room, I see there's nothing left to throw or break aside from Hudson's laptop.

Chairs and tables are strewn about, legs broken and jagged

pieces scattered throughout.

As soon as the men of WRATH released me, I tore into everything within reach. Slammed and punched until the violence subsided to a manageable level.

"I'm saying it was a fake. My guy is saying he never signed such an order and the kids' social worker has no clue what's going on." Hudson's eyes are calm, the complete opposite of what I'm feeling.

"So he took her. The motherfucker stole her and the kids. But why?" My hands fly up to my scalp, the fingers tugging at the hair.

Just then, Leventhal's associate rushes in followed by Aiden and Titus. "We think you need to see this."

They throw a briefcase onto the couch, and as soon as Hudson opens it my body goes cold. "Is that what I think it is?"

Hudson looks up at me and nods. "Looks like receipts for wire transfers. All from Mexico."

"The cartel. This fucker was working with the cartel." I whirl around, rounding on the trembling play therapist. "You. Did you know?"

"Oh god no. I had no clue until I went searching for a file." She's visibly shaking, Titus and Aiden at either side of her, making sure I don't crack and do something I can't take back.

Good men. At this point, I don't even trust myself.

Turning back to Hudson, I demand action. "So what now? How do we get them back?"

The men of WRATH look at each other before Hudson speaks. "There's no we, Jack. You can't come with us."

"Like hell I fucking can't. That's my girl. Those are my

kids." I start pacing in front of him, trying to figure out a way to convey that there is no other way. "They are my world, Hudson. Either you let me come with you or I'll find someone else who will."

He looks past me to his brothers, only speaking once Aiden has given him the nod of approval. "Fine, but if you're coming with us, then you need to do everything we say. We can't risk losing the mission because we're focused on keeping you alive."

I nod in full agreement. "The kids come first. Whatever happens, they come first."

Hudson gives me a curt nod when his radio goes off. Bringing it to his ear, his eyes go wide. "Roger that. We're on our way."

He stands, picking up his laptop and heading out the door. "We're rolling out. They've got eyes on the kids. Amanda and Alex are at a church about five miles from here."

Amanda and Alex. But not Pen. My stomach sinks, not wanting to think the worst but despite my trying, my mind wanders as visions of Pen being raped and brutalized flood me.

I'm making a choked sound when Hudson's hand lands on my shoulder. "Snap out of it, brother. We'll get her back. In the meantime, the kids need you."

I shake my head clear of the visions and start walking. He's right. The kids need me and I can't fail them. Falling apart or not, I need to pull my shit together and be their rock.

I call out to Mary as we step out the door, her answering voice letting me know she's within earshot.

"Please get your granddaughter here. I'll take care of any

expenses. Just get her here fast. I'm going to need help with the kids and the more eyes on them, the better."

Her matronly frame is now standing at the door, her white hair bobbing up and down in agreement. "Yes, sir. Of course."

With a nod of gratitude, I turn and follow Hudson into one of the blacked out SUVs.

It's time to get my kids.

Chapter Twenty-Nine

PENELOPE

The scent of roses hits me as I roll to my side. *Roses?*

I try to open my eyes, but they're caked shut, my head throbbing as I try to remember how I got here.

Taking my fingers, I rub at my lids, forcefully prying them open despite my head protesting the light.

What in the world?

I'm in a room. *No, a damn suite.* Laid out on a massive canopy bed, the thick fabric surrounding me doing nothing to block out the daylight.

Looking down at my body, I see that I'm no longer in a towel, and instead I have on a pale yellow sundress. Oh, god. Someone dressed me. Someone saw me naked. *Did they touch*

I need to get out of here, fast. Stepping down off of the mountain of blankets and pillows, I see an enormous vase of yellow roses on a bedside table. It's so huge the circumference of the bouquet takes up all the space.

Coming closer, I inspect it for a card, but there's nothing. No sign of who it's from or why it's here.

Spinning around, I see that the room is nothing short of opulent. The art on the walls, the oriental rugs on the floor. It all screams money.

Whoever brought me here has a shit ton of it. Way more than the Crown brothers.

Fear settles deep in my gut. Surely, whoever has this kind of money has the power to keep me hidden. My knees wobble, threatening to give out.

I need to get out of here. Rushing to a set of French doors, I pull them open, only to be met with the most amazing bathroom I've ever seen. It puts Jack's *en-suite* to shame.

Marble floors cover the entire room with a beautiful vanity situated right in the middle with designer cosmetics displayed perfectly for use. *Is all of this for me?*

Curiosity gets the better of me and I walk further into the bathroom. Seeing there's a smaller set of French doors to the right, I pull them open and gasp.

The walk-in wardrobe is full to the brim, every imaginable piece of wardrobe hanging there like some sort of designer boutique. Stepping in, I let a hand caress all of the gorgeous Yves Saint Laurent heels. Every one in my size.

Freaked out but curious, I pull a drawer open and see silk undergarments in every neutral shade. Pulling a bra closer, my eyes practically bug out when I see that it's also in my exact size.

Dropping the offending piece, I run out of the wardrobe and back into the room. Heading straight to the only other doors, I pull one open and come to a screeching halt when I see an armed man standing there. He's dressed in all black, his sunglasses hiding his eyes and concealing his intent.

As soon as he sees me, his hand flies up to his ear and he presses something before speaking. "She's up."

Dropping his hand, he gives me a broad smile. "If you're ready, miss. I'll take you to your father."

My breath hitches and all air leaves my lungs. "What—What did you just say?"

Surely, I must be hallucinating. This shit can't be real. I don't have a father.

"Your father, miss. I was instructed to take you to him as soon as you awoke. That is, unless you'd rather freshen up beforehand." His face flushes, making this moment even more absurd. Here is this looming figure with guns strapped to either side of his frame, and he's…. blushing. "Marta, the head maid, dressed you, but you can change if you wish. She placed everything you'll need in the en suite."

I'm standing there blinking, dumbfounded. So those things *were* for me. Bought for me at my *father's* request.

Not even wanting to know how he knows my cup size, I simply shake my head. "No, that won't be necessary."

"Okay. Please follow me." The man walks down the hallway, and I do as he says. I follow.

Not because I'm some obedient little girl, but because I need to get this production over with as soon as possible so I can get home. Get to wherever Alex and Amanda are.

This man who thinks he's my father, he's wrong. It's not possible, and the sooner he sees that, the sooner he lets me go.

We step into a main hall and I see that the opulence hasn't stopped at my room. No, it's carried throughout this entire villa. Calling it anything else would be a disservice to its beauty.

I wonder if we're in the States anymore.

Looking at my guard, I quirk a brow. "Where are we?"

"Your father will answer that." He steps aside and motions me into a room. "This way."

The door opens and I see a massive figure silhouetted by the sun. He's standing in front of a window, looking out into what I can now see is the ocean.

My guard speaks, making me jolt where I stand. "Sir, your daughter."

The imposing man slowly turns and his familiar eyes land on mine. I know those eyes. I see them every morning when I look in the mirror. My brows are pushing together as the door behind me clicks shut.

"Please sit." The man motions to the chair, and I do as he says, but only for fear of falling if I stand any longer.

I'm blinking up at him when his words hit me straight in the chest. "I'm so sorry for your loss, princess."

Not only has he used the term of endearment Jack has given me, but he's speaking of my loss. My mother. Austin. *How does he know?*

He takes the wingback chair next to mine, his elbows dropping to his knees as he blows out a long breath. "This isn't how I pictured our meeting. I'm not in the business of saying sorry, but in this case I truly am."

I keep blinking, wondering if I'm going to wake up any minute and see that this is all some bizarre dream. "Please don't call me that. I'm not your princess and you're not my daddy."

"You will always be my princess, Penelope, and I will always be your daddy." The man sits back in his chair, unfazed by my words. If anything, he seems pleased with my grit. "You look just like her, but you have my eyes. I didn't know what to think when word reached me that my rival cartel had you. I swear I've never felt such fear and anger, all for a child I had no idea existed."

Rival cartel. His words filter through my confusion, something mom said before she died falling into place. In a flash of black, I'm taken back to that room, the scent of copper filling my nose.

She tries to drag her beaten body over to me, attempting to use herself as a human shield. But she's too weak after her last beating and every move she makes is accompanied with a full-body flinch.

"Dumb bitch." The man pulls Mom up by her hair, placing the barrel of his gun to her temple.

"You're the dumb bitch." Mom spits in his face, the bold action earning her a punch to the ribs. Still, she gives the man shit, diverting his attention from me.

"Her father is going to have your head."

"Oh my god. You're my dad." I'm shaking, my hands trembling as I run my palms up and down my thighs, trying to calm myself. "She knew this whole time, and she never told me the truth. All she said was that you walked out and wanted nothing to do with us."

"Seems like she was lying to the both of us. No. She never told me about you and the only reason I found out you existed was because my rival cartel thought to use you as a bargaining chip. They knew they were in deep water with me and their time was coming near. When your mom mentioned my name and said I was your father, they kept you alive." He runs a hand over his tired features, his jaw working behind his scarred fingers. Now that I'm truly looking, I see it. The familiarity of his features. There's no denying it. He's my father. "I suppose I could see why she hid you from me. She didn't want this kind of life for you."

He stands, his feet carrying him over to a bar in the corner where he fills a rocks glass with amber liquid. "No matter. You're here now. This is where you belong. You're the heir to the Cardenas throne. Our very own cartel princess."

My eyes go wide, my mind reeling with what he's just said. "Oh, no. I'm no princess. I'm just a normal girl. A girl who lives in Colorado with her brother and sister." My throat constricts as my mouth goes dry. "Amanda and Alex, what did you do with them? Where are they?"

He nods, a smile playing on his lips as he brings his glass to his mouth, not answering me until he's had a sip. "Loyal, I see. That's a good trait for my successor." He walks back to the window, giving me his back, proving that he's not afraid of me or what I can do. "They're safe. Last I heard, they were back in the care of this *Jack*."

He says his name like it's the gum beneath his shoe. "How

do I know you're not lying?"

My father turns to me, a wide smile splayed across his face. "I should have known that a Cardenas would demand proof. You are my daughter, after all. Hell, I had that doctor swipe your hairbrush just so we could run a DNA test, making sure Blanca wasn't lying."

My mouth drops open at this revelation. I knew I didn't misplace my damn hairbrush. "Fine. The apple doesn't fall far from the tree. So show me. Show me my brother and sister are okay."

He raises a brow but says nothing, simply walks around his desk to a laptop that's cracked open. Pressing a couple of buttons, he finds what he's looking for and turns the screen so it's facing me.

There, as clear as day, I see Amanda and Alex running into Jacks' arms. A church I've never seen before in the background.

Pulling me from the screen, my father clears his throat. "I give you my word that they are safe and being watched over. No harm will come to them."

My face heats remembering the men who took us in Mexico. "But your rival cartel, they're still after us." My hands go to either side of my face, running through scenarios where both Amanda and Alex are taken from Jack. Hell, my dad did it, so who's to say they can't. Panic consumes me as I press my hands onto my father's desk. "They killed Mom and Austin. They won't stop until they get them too."

My father's eyes close, his face taking on a pained expression. "Like I said, I'm so sorry for Blanca. I wish I could've saved her, but I was away on business. As for the kids, you don't have to worry, *princessa*. The men that hurt you, that took your mother, they're all dead. And the ones that worked for them, we got them too." A glint of evil flashes across his face before a wicked smile forms on his lips. "Those *pendejos* thought they were real smooth, hunting you down in Colorado, but they weren't counting on the fact that I had someone on the inside. As soon as we discovered their location, my men went in and handled it. *Nobody fucks with a Cardenas.*"

A shiver runs through me, not even wanting to think about what his version of handling things looks like.

Not wanting any part of this, I walk backwards until my knees bump against my chair, lowering myself onto it before I topple over from all of this information. "But I don't belong here. I belong home, in Colorado."

Darkness falls over his features. "You are Daniel Cardenas' daughter. You're my daughter. You're the cartel princess and you will be staying here. This is your home now." He stands and walks to the door, opening it wide before turning around to address me. "Marco here will take you back to your room until you've settled down. I understand this is a lot of information for you to take in, but you *will* take it and you *will* step up to your duties as my only living flesh and blood. You are a Cardenas and I won't let you forget it."

Without another word, he steps into the hallway, leaving me gawking after him with only the company of my guard.

Marco steps to my side, waiting for me to rise. I do, because there's no sense in me staying here. Not when I have an escape plan to hatch.

FILTHY CROWN

Chapter Thirty
JACK

Two damn weeks and not a single lead. I'm pacing back and forth in my study, waiting. I'm always fucking waiting, coming out of my skin, begging God for just a glimmer of hope.

There's a knock on my door, pulling me from my thoughts. "Come in," I growl.

"The kids asleep?" Matt steps in, followed by Hunter and Jace.

"Yes, Anaya got them down about thirty minutes ago." Truth be told, Mary's granddaughter has been a blessing to us. Without her, I wouldn't be able to focus so much time on searching for Pen.

"That girl has taken to her role as nanny like a fish to water," Jace adds while pouring himself a drink.

"Yeah, but we might have to send her away despite that." Matt raises a brow, his gaze landing on me. "Y'all know how Jack has a taste for the younger ones. Hate to see that innocent girl get trapped in his web."

I'm about to lunge at Matt for the horribly inappropriate comment when Hunter steps in, holding me back. "Fucking asshole. I love Pen, and you damn well know it."

Hunter, refusing to let me go, speaks up behind me, "That was a cheap shot, Matt. Especially since Pen made her position clear on the situation."

Matt's about to speak up when there's a knock on the door.

"Come in," we all say in unison.

Titus and Hudson step in, a guarded expression on their face.

Letting out a shaky breath, I steel myself for the worst. "Out with it. What info do you have?"

"We're going to need y'all to come with us." Titus is serious, not an ounce of emotion betraying whatever he's hiding.

My eyes narrow, not wanting to play any games. "Just spit it out. Where are we going? Did you find Pen?"

Hudson speaks, "It's not about Pen, though we have a lead on her whereabouts. This is about Austin."

My head cocks back, but it's Jace who speaks up. "Austin?"

Titus claps down a hand on his shoulder. "Yes. He's alive."

Murmurs, gasps and a set of curse words are heard around the room as my legs threaten to give out. *"Holymotherfuckingshit.* Where is he? Take us to him. Now!"

Titus raises a brow at my demand, the rest of his face still stoic as ever. "That's what we were doing until you started asking all these questions."

"Oh, I still have plenty of questions. But we can ask them on the way." I move toward the door, all Crown brothers following suit. "I'll just let Anaya know we're leaving. Meet everyone outside in five."

My leg bounces impatiently, willing this SUV to go faster. "So, you just found him wandering in the Mexican desert?"

Titus is driving, his eyes focused on the road. "Yes. Our men were doing recon on the Las Cruces cartel when they stumbled upon him."

Hudson turns from the front passenger seat, his face apologetic. "He's in rough shape. Extremely emaciated, and frankly, it's a damn miracle he's still alive."

"I bet it was sheer will to see his babies once more that kept him going," I mumble under my breath, knowing that Pen is the only driving force behind every breath I take now. Without her, I have nothing.

As if reading my mind, Hunter places a hand on my shoulder. "We'll find her."

"Thank you, brother." I feel like a dick, not being able to fully appreciate Austin being found, but Pen is my world and my soul will never be complete without her.

"The report you gave us said his body was found during your rescue mission. How could that be if he's now here in Texas?" Matt asks from behind us.

"Austin had beat up one of the guards, divested him of his clothes and switched places, but not before removing the man's head." Hudson's jaw clenches as he stares Matt down.

"*Jesus Christ*," Jace mutters under his breath. "Who knew Austin had that in him?"

"From what we've gathered, that's how he escaped. His plan was to get out and get help." Matt turns, facing out the window once more. "Too bad for him, the Villa was surrounded by nothing but deserted land. The cartel wasn't exactly keen on neighbors. Not with all the shit they were doing on that compound."

The SUV comes to a stop in front of a nondescript building. Apparently, this is an outpatient facility where the men of WRATH bring their clients in order to avoid media scrutiny. It's brilliant, making me realize once more that these guys are worth every damn penny.

After passing a ton of security checkpoints, we're finally outside of Austin's room. Hudson's hand falls to the doorknob, his eyes floating over all four Crown brothers before opening it and beckoning us inside.

My eyes water as they fall on our brother, his body a shadow of what it once was. "*Jesus.*"

Austin's eyes flash up to mine, his lips turning up into a smirk as my other brothers surround his bed. "What? Don't like what you see?"

I let out a hoarse chuckle. "Good to see you've still got your sense of humor. You're going to need it."

Austin's eyes turn dark, falling on Hudson who's still lingering by the door. "I know. They've told me the news about Pen."

A lump lodges in my throat, hearing her name fall from his

lips. "I'm sorry, Austin."

His eyes return to mine, the room stilling when a ragged sob falls from his mouth. "It's my fault. It's all my fucking fault."

I collapse onto the bed, pulling him into me. "Shh. Don't say that. Don't say that, brother. We'll get her back. Everything is going to be okay. I swear to you on all that I hold dear, I will find a way to get her back."

Hunter, Matt, and Jace all fall onto us—giving into a group hug, the likes we haven't seen since our childhood years.

Right there, in the massive tangle of limbs and tears, I vow over and over again to never stop searching. I'm thankful for our brother coming back to us, but there's no way we'll ever be complete without Pen.

Chapter Thirty-One

PENELOPE

It's been over a month and with every passing day, my hope for rescue or escape fades along with the setting sun.

I'm getting ready to get out of bed when a wave of nausea hits me. Rushing to the toilet, I make it just in time to empty last night's dinner into the bowl.

My stomach is used to the water here in Mexico, so I know it's not that. And the food we get is nothing but the best. My father wouldn't allow subpar anything, let alone food for his precious little heir.

Another wave of nausea hits me and I brush my hair aside, making sure to avoid it getting covered in puke. As I'm heaving into the toilet, one word keeps blaring loud and in neon letters

That has to be it. Jack and I didn't use any protection, and despite my captivity, I've been keeping track of my cycle. I'm over a week late and now this.

Getting up from the floor, I walk over to the sink, turning the tap on and splashing my face.

Looking into the mirror, I wonder how different things would be if I were back home with Jack. Would he still be trying to ship me off to college? Our last time in the shower plays in my head and my stomach churns.

The way we left things was horrible. He lied. He promised he would always be there, but then he pushed me away on some bullshit claim that it's what was best for me.

Anger makes my skin flush, but I push it aside. No matter now. The life inside me is more important than my feelings. I may never let him in my bed again, but my child deserves to know what it's like to have a father. I could never let it grow up the way I did.

It's okay. Everything will be okay. We will get through this.

Staring into the mirror, I see my father's eyes staring back in my own.

It's time he and I had a talk. Daniel Cardenas may be a cruel cartel leader, but there's no way he'd deny his own grandchild this.

Getting a hold of my resolve, I straighten my nightgown and pull on a robe, determined to have him hear me out.

I open the bathroom door, stepping into my bedroom and freeze. *A ghost.* That's the only explanation.

"Austin?" I whisper as I walk toward the male figure before me.

"Shhh. Pen. I'll get you out of here." He's pressing a finger to his lips, trying to get me to stay quiet.

"But you're *dead*." The last word comes out with a squeak, the sound enough to alert the guard outside my door.

It flings open and two men rush in, training a gun on Austin. On instinct, I fling myself toward him. "No, you can't!"

"Miss Cardenas, step away from the intruder." One of the men pleads in a calm voice, but I don't move.

"No! He's my stepdad. You can't shoot him. I won't let you."

Both men look at each other, the one in the back speaking into his earpiece.

The room is stock-still, waiting for someone to move when the guy in the back speaks. "The boss wants to see him."

"Not without me." I hold on to Austin as if my life depended on it. I've just got him back and there's no way I'm letting go.

He strokes the back of my hair, his lips landing on the top of my head. "It's okay, Pen. Everything will be okay."

I choke back a sob, the mixture of hormones and the emotional high of seeing a man I thought dead becoming too much. "No. It won't. Not unless I come with you"

Austin nods, but looks toward the guards for confirmation. The larger one nods in agreement. Thank god, because I was ready to put up a fight and considering my current state, I'd probably just end up puking all over everyone.

Grabbing onto Austin's arm, I walk us out into the hall and down toward my dad's office. "This is fine. Everything's going to be fine." I absently pat my stepdad's hand, wondering if it really will be okay.

Maybe now is when I should drop the news. Use the surprise

of a new life to our advantage. A hand goes to my abdomen. *Ready or not, peanut. Here we go.*

The double doors open into the study and for the second time today, I'm frozen in place.

The Crown brothers along with Titus and Hudson are all seated around the conference table, my father at the head, holding up a rocks glass as if in mid toast. "Ah, *Princessa.* You've made it just in time."

My mouth is hanging open, my eyes wide with wonder. "What's going on here?"

Jack's eyes find mine, full of so much emotion. I'm about to run straight to him when one of the guards places their hand on my shoulder, keeping me in place.

My father speaks up, "Austin, why don't you join us at the table. *Princessa,* you come here, stand by my side where you belong."

Seeing as he's the one with all the power and possibly all the guns right now, I do as he says. My feet swiftly carry me to his side, my eyes going back to Jack and seeing that his jaw is clenched and fist balled up over the mahogany table.

My hand goes to my abdomen and I find the courage needed to confront my father. "What's going on, Dad?" I turn to him and give him a placid smile, not wanting him tipped off that I'm truly rattled. If he's taught me anything, it's how to handle a room full of powerful men.

"I was just having a chat here with the Crown brothers and their security. I'm really impressed with how far they got onto my property. So much so that I've *removed* some of my men and have asked them to step in and plug any holes in our coverage here at the Villa." He looks at the men, a genuine smile on his lips.

Jack speaks up, and hearing his voice for the first time in months shakes me to my core. "And like I said, we came here for Pen. Our men will gladly help you with whatever you need as long as she comes home with us."

All of the men seem unfazed by Austin's presence, and I can only assume that he came here with them. I'll definitely need the details of that later.

I'm staring at my stepfather when my father speaks. "And like I said, she's the heir to the Cardenas' throne. She will marry one of my men soon, and she and her partner will take over my business. Surely, you all are family men. You can see why letting her go is not an option."

"I can't marry one of your men, Father." A lump rises in my throat, the courage I had once is now ebbing away. As all eyes land on mine, I lay it all on the line. "I'm with child, and the baby's father is at this table."

My father's eyes go wide as Jack releases a choked sound, earning him Daniel's ire. "Is this true? Is it *yours*?"

Jack's face blanches, but it's quickly replaced with a massive grin. "Holy *fucking* shit. I'm going to be a father."

My dad smacks his hand on the table. "Marco, break out the Cardenas' Reserve. Looks like we have a celebration on our hands."

Marco makes haste, heading off somewhere before quickly returning with a bottle of my father's own tequila.

Jack is now walking toward me, his arms pulling me into an embrace as his lips reach the top of my head.

A sob is pulled from my lips and despite my best efforts to remain stoic in front of my father, I crumble in my man's arms.

"God, Princess. I've missed you so fucking much," Jack murmurs into my hair, only being cut off by my father clearing his throat.

"We will celebrate but then will discuss the new heir born into this family."

Jack bristles at my father's words. "With all due respect Don Cardenas, this child will be a Crown and he will carry our name."

My father stands, not one to be in any position of inferiority, and that includes stature as Jack and I stand next to him. "I am fully aware that this is your offspring, but this is my daughter, and I require an heir to my empire. This pairing is not one of my choosing, but I will not deny my grandchild a father. He will not suffer like my daughter did."

Daniel's eyes fall on mine and I do my best to convey my gratitude for this understanding.

"That said, I will leave the ball in your court. Penelope may go home with you and have her child, with my added protection, of course. She will have a family with you, but in turn, you will train with me and my men. Jack, I'm offering you the keys to my kingdom."

Jack's about to respond, but my father holds up a hand, making him hold his tongue. "Before you give me your answer, you have to understand that the only other option I will agree to is for my *princessa* to stay here. One of my men will gladly step up to the plate and be the child's father. She'll marry him and he'll never know the meaning of being a bastard. Of that you have my word."

Jack tenses beside me, save for his jaw, which is ticking. I pull his hand into mine, squeezing his fingers and silently begging him to accept. My eyes find his, and they well up with tears. I couldn't survive without him and as his eyes search mine, I know he sees my truth.

"I agree to take over your businesses, but I have terms of my own." Jack pulls me to him, his hand stroking my back in soothing circles as I let out a breath I didn't know I was holding.

My father nods. "Of course. I'd expect as much from a man like you. Any less and I wouldn't deem you worthy of my daughter." He raises his fresh glass, full of Cardenas tequila, handing Jack one of his very own. "To family."

Everyone around the table raises their glass and cheers in unison, "To family."

Chapter Thirty-Two

PENELOPE

S tepping into the foyer, I let out a breath of relief. We're back at the ranch. Never in a million years did I think I'd be coming back here, pregnant with Jack's baby.

Heck, there was a time where I wasn't sure I'd be setting foot here ever again.

Now that I've had time to process everything we've been through, I stand firm on my decision. I'll let Jack be the father of this baby, he can even run my father's businesses, but I will not let him in my heart again.

I still don't know the details of what was discussed between Daniel and Jack, and frankly, I don't want to know. What I do want to know is how Austin survived.

I'm about to go in search of answers when two small figures

almost topple me to the ground.

"Careful," Jack's voice booms from behind me. His hands steady me, my treacherous body lighting up at the contact. "Your sister is carrying precious cargo."

I turn back to him and glare. I wanted to be the one to tell them, on my own time.

Alex looks between Jack and me. "Cargo?"

Lowering myself down to them, I whisper. "It's a secret I'll tell you about later. For now, how about you give me a great big hug? I've missed you two so much."

They do as asked, letting me pull them into an embrace that can only be described as home. "We missed you too, Pen."

Pulling away, I see Alex's eyes are wet and Amanda is outright crying. "Shh. Dry those eyes. Everything is going to be okay." My eyes look out the window to see that the SUV carrying Austin and the other Crown brothers has just pulled up. "Look who's here?"

I jerk my head outside and the kids' eyes go wide. "Daddy!" They beeline it to the door as a beautiful blonde steps out from the hallway.

I tilt my head, waiting to place her, or at the very least get an introduction.

Jack speaks up first. "This is Mary's granddaughter, Anaya. She's been helping with the kids while we handled things in Mexico."

I owe this woman a great deal if she's managed to keep the little nuggets content all this time. They just got their dad back and then he up and left again on a rescue mission for me. I can't imagine what their little hearts have been through.

Rising to my feet, I extend a hand. "So nice to meet you, Anaya. Thank you so much for all that you've done. I honestly couldn't thank you enough."

Her already rosy complexion turns a deeper shade of pink. "No worries, miss. It's been a pleasure. Those two have the biggest heart."

"I'm glad you like your job, because I'll be asking you to stay on," Jack speaks beside me and an irrational spark of jealousy hits me straight in the gut, only settled by his next words. "Austin will stay here at the ranch while he undergoes therapy and once finished, he'll be helping take over the business."

He glances at me and that's when I realize this must've been part of his agreement with my dad.

Just then Austin walks in with the kids, his eyes landing on the young blonde, his face paling and his eyes blinking several times before he actually speaks. "Anaya. Hello."

Okay. *That's interesting.*

Turning to look at the girl, I see that deep shade of pink has returned. "Sir, welcome home."

Austin clears his throat, dismissing the nanny without a response before turning to the kids and giving her his back. "Kids, why don't you show me what you've been up to while Daddy was away?"

Amanda hops up and down while Alex's face splits into a wide grin. "Yes, dad. You have to see the model airplane I've been working on."

"And my dolly. I cut her hair and made her all pretty." Amanda squeals, not wanting to be left out.

With both kids in hand, Austin gives us all a wide smile. "I'll see y'all for dinner. I'm off to spend some time with my kids."

Jack nods, his hand dropping to my lower back and making me still.

As soon as everyone's cleared the foyer, I whirl on Jack. "Don't touch me."

He rears his head back in surprise. "What are you talking about? I touched you in Mexico, in front of a freaking cartel boss, risking my life by showing his only heir affection. And now? Now you deny me a simple touch?"

I let out a shaky breath, knowing I have a fight ahead of me. "It seems we have some things to discuss. Some ground rules to set."

"Ground rules," Jack repeats, his eyes narrowing before motioning down the hall. "By all means, let's go to my study and discuss these ground rules."

I lead the way, walking back through the familiar walls. God, how I missed this place. It's crazy to see how much of a home it became in just a few weeks.

"Talk." Jack closes the door behind us, his steps carrying him to his bar where he pours himself some Tortured Crown whiskey.

I sit down in one of the wingback chairs, not wanting to give him the option to sit next to me. "I'm still mad at you. You lied to me. Said you wouldn't leave me and then, after fucking me, you went back on your word. You abandoned me just like you did four years ago." My teeth clench and my breathing picks up. I will not cry. I will not let him see how much he hurt me. "I won't deny you your child, and given the circumstances surrounding who I really am, I'm okay with marrying you and pretending to be a family for the sake of our kid and for my father. But that's it."

"That's it?" Jack scoffs, slamming down the tumbler on his desk, spilling whiskey all over the sleek wood. He rushes toward me, grabbing me by the arms and pulling me to standing.

In one fell swoop, he's raised me off the floor, his arms dropping to cradle my ass, holding me up so that his face is a breath away from mine. "Listen here, . I'm not happy with how things went down. I'm not perfect, far from it. But I didn't abandon you. I didn't leave you. I said I would always be here for you and I fucking meant it."

My hands push at his shoulders, trying to shove him away so he'll put me down, but it's futile. He's stronger, and he's not putting me down until we're through with this conversation. *Fine.*

I drop my hands, resting them on my chest, refusing to touch him. "You said, and I quote 'Daddy's got you and he's never letting you go.' But you abandoned me when you told me we could no longer be... no longer claim me as yours. I could never forget your actions. Not when I was a broken little girl waiting by the window, and definitely not now, as a grown woman."

His forehead drops onto mine, his exhale warming my lips and making me shiver. "Princess. Sometimes daddies fuck up. They think they know what's best for their little girls, but they're only human. I'm only human." He lifts his forehead from mine, pressing a soft kiss to my lips. "Baby, I promise I thought I was doing what was best for you. There isn't any part of me that wanted to let you go. I was doing it for you. Everything I've done since you first set foot on this ranch has been for you."

Jack's arms shift so his hands are directly on my ass, urging my legs to wrap around him. My eyes find his, trying to find the truth in them, wondering if I should expose myself again to this man who has held my heart for longer than I'd care to admit, and deep down inside, I know he still does.

His nose rubs against mine, our breath mingling and setting my soul on fire.

"Jack, I can't. My heart. It won't survive it again."

"Time, ." He presses a soft peck to my lips. "I ask for time. Let me show you you're my everything. That you mean the world to me. I was wrong, Pen. I now know that your place has always been by my side. It was stupid of me to think I knew what was best for you based on what an ordinary teenager needs. You're the farthest thing from it. You're extraordinary. A woman who's lived the life of three, one who, despite life's dealings, still holds an amazing capacity for love, loyalty, and I know for me—understanding."

What he's saying makes sense. I know he's right. He's human, and I can see and feel the love he says he has. It's like a live current between us, obvious to anyone within our orbit.

"Time." I repeat. "I can do time."

Jack presses a hard kiss to my lips, whispering as he lets me slide off his body. "Thank you, . I promise to make you the happiest woman alive."

I quirk a brow. "That's quite the promise, Daddy."

His lips turn up into a full grin and I can't help but giggle as I walk out of his study. Teasing him all over again is going to be all sorts of delicious fun.

Now, priorities. I need to find Mary and see if she'll make me some of those cinnamon rolls. I've been craving those for weeks and this baby isn't taking no for an answer.

Chapter Thirty-Three

JACK

It's been two months since Mexico, and everything is so different.

For starters, Austin has been staying at the ranch. Between Pen and Mary's granddaughter, he's had all the help he needs with the kids, giving him time to recover from the mental scars that wandering the Mexican desert caused.

I'm not going to lie, it was quite a shock seeing him after thinking he'd been dead. It was great news, but shocking nonetheless.

The men of WRATH found him roaming around in the Mexican desert, trying to find his way back to his kids. He was a dehydrated mess, but once he physically recovered, there wasn't anything that could hold him back from going after Pen.

Now that we're home, he's back to working on himself

Despite his amazing physical recovery, he still needs help with the emotional trauma. Thankfully, the men of WRATH have been able to help with that transition, setting him up with a therapist that's been fully vetted.

Although the situation with Pen and Dr. Leventhal worked out in the end, there's no way we'll be taking that sort of risk again. It was by sheer luck that no harm came to her, only made possible by the fact that the Cartel leader who hired Leventhal was Pen's biological father. The chances of that happening again are non-existent.

Even so, Austin still feels guilty for everything that went down with the Las Cruces cartel—especially for Blanca—and frankly, it's the only reason he hasn't torn me to shreds over having touched his stepdaughter, let alone claiming her as mine.

And Pen. *Oh, Pen.*

She's been a handful, that's for sure. With Jackson Crown, Jr. set to arrive in six months, Pen's curves have only gotten fuller and all the more tempting. It's taken everything in me to give her the space and time she needs, and I'm hanging on by a thread.

"Sir, everything's ready," Sam calls from the door and I get up from my desk where I'd been staring aimlessly at my computer screen.

"Thank you, Sam. I'm hoping this does the trick." I let out a breath while running a hand down my face, praying that this is enough for her to see that I mean what I say.

Sam pats me on the shoulder, a broad smile playing on his lips. "Sir, if you don't mind my saying. I think Miss Penelope forgave you a long time ago. That girl is head over heels in love with you, and at this point, I think she's just busting your balls because it's fun."

I narrow my eyes at him but know that there's probably some truth to that. "We'll see."

Leaving Sam behind, I go in search of Pen. I've played her little games long enough. Now it's time to make her mine.

Penelope

Two months. Two *long-ass* months of pure-*fucking*-torture.

Watching Jack strut around the house in his tight shirts and gray sweatpants has my lady bits about to shrivel up and die. I know it's my own doing. I should've forgiven him a long time ago, but what can I say… I'm stubborn and proud as hell.

At this point, it'd be obvious to a blind man that I'm Jack's forever. The way he dotes on me, making sure I have everything I need and never once letting me go without, speaks volumes. To top it all off, his caveman possessive ways have come out in full force now that I'm pregnant. He needs to know where I am at all times and doesn't let me go outside a two-mile radius unless he's by my side.

Yeah. It's clear that man isn't letting me go.

As I let out a shaky sigh, my body tingles with need, remembering him in the hallway without a shirt—freshly showered with drops of water still clinging to his bare chest. *Lord have mercy.* Bringing the glass of Mary's lemonade to my lips, I take a sip, my throat having suddenly gone dry. *Yeah. It's time.*

I'm sitting on the porch swing about to go in search of my man, when a large figure steps in front of me, as if I've conjured him with my very mind.

"We're leaving." Jack takes the glass from my hands and places it on the wooden railing behind him.

"Oh, are we now? And what if I don't want to go?" Blinking up at him in surprise, I can't help but sass him.

"Too bad." He leans down, his muscular arms picking me up bridal style and carrying me over to a four-seater ATV. "We've played things nice and slow for a while now. But I'm over it. You're mine, always have been. I see it. Your stepfather sees it. Your biological father sees it. Hell, even the damn dog sees it."

"We don't have a dog, Jack." I giggle in his arms as he lowers me into the passenger seat, making sure I'm buckled up.

"But if we did, he'd fucking see it too." He raises a brow, the soft smile on his lips begging me to argue.

I remain quiet as he rounds the ATV to the driver's seat, knowing he's one-hundred percent correct. "That's what I thought. Now be a good girl and let Daddy take you for a ride."

At his words, my pussy throbs and my lips suck in a sharp breath. Unable to stay still, my bottom wiggles against the seat, betraying what I really feel. Yeah. It's no secret I want him. No, scratch that. I *need* him.

"Jack," I mewl, and it takes a strength I didn't know I possessed to keep my hands to myself. If I touch him now, there's no guarantee I won't jump him right in front of the house.

"Just you wait, Princess. What I've got in store for you..." Jack's words die off as he pulls out and heads to god-knows-where. All I know is that we need to get there, and fast.

After what seems like hours, we finally reach our destination, the cabin where I first climbed him like a tree. A blush heats my face at the memory. God, what I'd give to feel him between my thighs again.

Stepping out of the ATV, I'm immediately taken aback, my eyes going wide at the carpet of pink and red rose petals blanketing a path toward a trail I know all too well.

"Oh my God, Jack. Did you do this?"

"I had Sam do it for us. Come, there's more to see." Grabbing my hand and interlacing our fingers, Jack walks us down the trail and out into an open space in front of the waterfall.

As soon as we've hit the clearing, my mouth drops open in surprise. I've only seen things like this on Pinterest. I didn't think people did this in real life.

Twinkle lights are strewn between the trees, creating a sparkling canopy for a massive blanket covered in pillows and votives. A knee-high table sits in the center, with a lone wicker basket sitting atop it.

"This is stunning," I whisper, unable to convey what I truly feel. Finally turning to Jack, I feel my eyes welling up with tears.

"I'm glad you like it. In full disclosure though, I might've gotten some pointers off the internet." He gives me a sheepish smile, but in truth, that doesn't matter to me. It's the thought that counts.

"So, what's this all for?" I shake my head and let out a nervous laugh. "Whatever it is, it must be really important."

He raises a brow before sweeping me off my feet, carrying

me to the blanket and placing me on one of the large pillows. "I told you. I'm tired of waiting."

"Oh, so this is your shot at seduction?" I smirk, giving him a hard time, but truth be told, I wouldn't object if he threw me down and had his way with me right here, right now.

"If I'm lucky, that'll come after. But the whole point of this is to make it clear to you, once and for all, that you are my everything and that I'm never leaving your side." Jack pulls open the picnic basket, handing me a set of papers that had been sitting inside.

"What's this?" My brows push together as I look down at the document, unsure of what this all means.

"It's a contract. I'm giving you everything that I own. Every cent, every square inch, and every stock. It's all yours. All you have to do is sign."

My mouth drops open in shock. "Jack. Have you lost your damn mind?"

"No. Never been clearer. There's no need for me to worry, because I'll always be by your side. I'm never leaving you, so I'll never be without." Before I can even respond, he maneuvers onto one knee, pulling out a little red box that makes my breath hitch. "Penelope Garcia, will you do me the honor of being my sugar momma?"

Oh. My. God.

My eyes fill with tears as the reality of what he's offering sinks in. He's willing to give up everything he owns, just so I'll feel safe in our relationship.

This strong man loves me to the point of selflessness and here I've been torturing him for the past two months, making him suffer because of my own emotional baggage.

Jack's face goes from hopeful to worried with every passing second I don't respond.

"Pen?" His eyes bounce back and forth between mine, begging for me to say yes.

I will. There's no doubt in my mind that I will be Mrs. Jack Crown, but I have to make something clear first.

Shifting off the pillow, I get onto my knees, holding out the contract and ripping it to shreds. "How dare you, Jack Crown? How dare you think I'd accept this?"

Jack's face falls as he gives me one curt nod, thinking he understands what I mean, but never being more wrong. "It's the only way I could think of showing you I meant what I said. That you are everything to me and without you I have nothing."

My hands push at his shoulders while big fat tears stream down my face. "You big dummy! Don't you see I already know that? I've always known that. It's me who should be sorry. Placing my trauma on you and making you work harder for my affection." I crawl onto his lap, my legs straddling him. "You've always wanted what was best for me. Even when you pushed me away, you were doing it for me. It was misguided but well intended, and I shouldn't have taken out my baggage on you. Could you forgive me?"

"God, Princess. There's nothing to apologize for." Jack's strong arms wrap around me, his hands pressing my chest into his. "Let's just say we both could have handled that a hell of a lot better and from now on, we'll talk shit out before rushing to make decisions. Deal?"

My tear-stained lips turn up into a smile, matching the one

on Jack's handsome face. "Deal. Now ask me again. Except skip the sugar momma part. I'd much rather you be my *daddy*."

His cock jumps at my words, bumping up against my ass and making me squirm. *Jesus.* That brief touch felt so damn good I can't help but groan, all while rolling my hips in search of more.

"Baby, if you keep moving like that, there won't be much more talking going on."

I throw my head back and laugh, knowing he's right. "Okay, okay. Go ahead and ask again. I promise I'll be good."

Jack brings one hand between us, his palm holding up the little red box. "Penelope Garcia, will you do me the honor of being my wife, my forever?"

"Yes! Yes! Oh my god, yes!" I fling my arms around his neck, peppering his face with kisses. The force of my pouncing has us toppling, Jack laid out on his back as I writhe against him.

"Thank god. One more second, and I wasn't above tying you up and using coercion." With one smooth move, Jack removes the ring from the box and places it on my finger, the weight of it on my hand feeling perfect.

With my palms on his chest, I prop myself up, admiring the large oval diamond sparkling in the light. "You know, tying me up could be fun, too."

Jack groans beneath me, his hard length pressing up between my folds and making me squirm. "Don't tease me with a good time, little girl."

"Oh, Daddy. Teasing means not following through…" I rotate my hips and bear down on him, pulling a deep rumble from his chest, "but I have every intention of finishing what I've started."

FILTHY CROWN

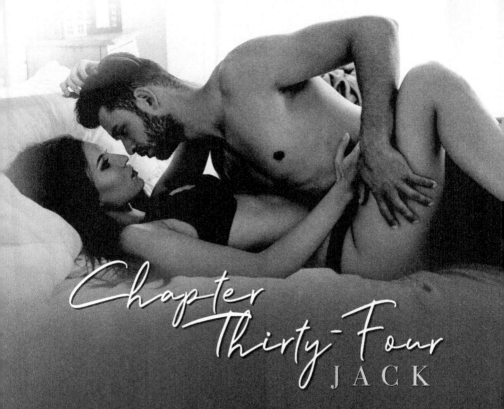

Chapter Thirty-Four
JACK

Like manna raining from above, her lips fall to mine, sating a deep hunger only she can quench. Greedy for more, I let my hands drop to her ass and squeeze, the round globes soft and pliable in my hold. *God, I missed her.*

I give her one hard thrust, bucking her into the air and making her squeak. "I need you right now, Princess."

Rolling her onto her back, I let my palms skim up the inside of her thighs; the action pulling up her summer dress and exposing her white lace panties, the patch in the middle already soaked through and clinging to her plump lips.

Fuck.

As if in a trance, my face comes down, tongue poking out and licking a line straight up her slit right over the thin fabric.

Pen lets out a mewl, bucking her hips upward, making my thick fingers dig into her soft thighs just to keep her in place.

"Stay still, Princess. Daddy wants a taste."

Placing an open-mouthed kiss to the top of her mound, I suck at her clit through the fabric, eliciting a guttural roar from my baby's lips.

"*Please*. No more teasing. Your dirty little girl can't take it anymore." Pen squirms in my hold, the urgency in her tone making me rut against a damn pillow. Truth is, I can't take any more of this torture either.

Getting onto my knees, I let her see what she's done to me— *what she always does to me.*

Slowly unzipping, I trail my eyes up her hot little body before landing on her pouty lips. "You know what to do, Princess. Open wide for Daddy."

Pen lets out a noise that has me pulsing in my hand. Her lithe body gets up to sitting, her tongue taking a slow thirsty swipe at her fat lower lip and I swear I almost come right then and there.

Eager to touch, Pen wraps one of her small hands around my girth, her pink tongue licking at the underside of my head, the action making me throw it back with a roar. "*Fuuuuuuck.*"

I'm still reeling from that one swipe when she shoves me deep into her mouth, taking me all the way back to her tight little throat and swallowing as much of me as she can, all while pumping the base.

She's gagging, her big hazel eyes looking up at me with such wonder, and I know my body can't hold out much longer.

I take both hands, fingers gripping onto either side of her head before pulling her off so that just the tip is sheathed inside.

Jesus. She's perfect. Zeroing in on her mouth, I slam back in and fuck her face with three hard thrusts.

My vision blurs and I know it's time to take her.

Pulling her off of me with a pop, I shove her back down onto a pillow. "Baby, I know I should be gentle. Do this nice and slow. But I can't." Ripping her panties clean off, I take myself in hand, slapping the tip of my cock against the top of her mound and reveling in every little noise I pull from her lips. Baring my teeth, I growl, "Daddy needs inside that pretty pussy."

"Please. Don't hold back..." Pen is panting now, her chest heaving toward me with every hard pull of breath. "Take me. Make me yours."

Her words flame the fire roaring through me, turning me into a savage beast as I rip down her dress, exposing her luscious tits, just begging for a taste. I need all of her as I take her. Claiming every golden inch of her glorious skin as mine.

Gripping one of her round breasts, I squeeze, marveling at how the perky flesh flushes around my fingers.

So. Damn. Beautiful.

Salivating, I bring my mouth down onto a pert nipple and suck. Her taste is like an explosion in my mouth, my eyes closing and memorizing the contours of the hard tip and saving it to the recesses of my mind.

I'm pressing my shaft against her slick folds, humping her tiny body with all that I have as I flick at her nipple with my tongue, the action driving Pen wild and making her reach for my dick.

"*Pleeeease,*" she whines, and I can deny her no longer. "I

need more." Pen reaches down, taking me into her hand and guiding me straight to heaven.

My bulbous tip, already leaking with precum, is now pressing at her slit, making her jerk violently. *"Oh god."*

Torturing me, she rubs the head up and down, circling it around her clit, her wide hips thrusting up into it. Unable to take any more, my hands go to her tiny waist and I watch my cock disappear into her heat as I shove myself into her with one hard ram.

"Faaaaaaaaak." I'm gasping for air, unable to catch my breath as the sensation of her walls clamping around me makes the rest of the world fade into oblivion.

There's only Pen and me. This wild connection we share, so clear in this moment, making everything technicolor. As if on some sort of sensory drug—every touch, every stroke, every squeeze of her pussy walls—feels heightened.

"Oh, Jack. *Daddy. Fuck.*" Pen's hands roam under my shirt, needing skin to skin.

Not wanting to deny us both, I rip the fabric off, exposing the hard planes of my body for her to touch.

Instantly, her nails dig a path down my abs, the mixture of pleasure and pain driving my hands right back to her waist as I buck into her tight warmth.

My eyes feast on her juicy tits as they bounce up and down with every thrust. Like two little sirens calling my mouth home, I bring my lips to one, sucking as much as I can into me before biting.

"Ohmyfuckinggod!" Pen's hands go to my back, her nails scratching down to my ass and gripping on for dear life.

I release her from my mouth, my tongue lapping at the tender flesh I've abused. "Fuck, baby. I want to eat you whole, take you into my body and keep you there."

My hands go to her round ass, keeping myself pressed against her as I lift one of her thighs and grind, rolling my hips until I'm hitting that spot inside her, driving her wild.

"I'm coming. Oh god, I'm coming." Pen's eyes squeeze shut, her body tensing in my hold. "*Mmmm, gaaahhh. So. Hard.*"

Taking my thumb, I bring it to her engorged clit and press, detonating a string of curse words from my filthy girl's mouth. "That's right, Princess. Milk Daddy's cock."

With each passing second, every flutter of her walls brings me closer to my own release. My balls tingle and my back aches, begging for completion. With one long roar, I let myself cum, tumbling down the waterfall of ecstasy with my girl.

Heaven. This is sheer fucking heaven, and there isn't anyone on this earth who can tell me otherwise.

I'm holding myself still, our hands gripping tightly onto one another as Pen continues to choke my cock, pulling every last spurt I have.

Looking down at her flushed face, my baby has never looked more beautiful. And to think, I get to have her for the rest of my life. "I love you, Pen. You're my damn world."

"I know." A wide grin spreads across her face, her eyes twinkling with so much adoration my chest can barely contain the flood of emotions this all brings. "I love you too. Always have and always will."

"Damn straight you will. You'll be a Crown soon." My fingers slip down to where we're still connected, coating them in our juices before bringing them to her mouth and painting her lips with the evidence of our love. "My very own *filthy-filthy* Crown."

I lower my mouth to hers, pulling her into a kiss that makes the world fade away once more. Come what may, she'll always be mine, and not a day will go by without my letting her know it.

Thank you for taking a chance on Filthy Crown. Please consider leaving a review if you enjoyed it. Reviews are like precious gold to authors and it would mean the world to me to hear what you thought of my book baby!

OTHER BOOKS
by Eleanor Aldrick

MEN OF WRATH SERIES (forbidden love):

ACTS OF ATONEMENT
age-gap/nanny/single dad

ACTS OF SALVATION
age-gap/best friend's uncle

ACTS OF REDEMPTION
Brother's best friend

ACTS OF GRACE
age-gap/Brother's Best Friend

CROWN SERIES (forbidden love):

FILTHY CROWN
age-gap/single dad/stepuncle

MAFIA ROMANCE:

OMERTA: A VERY MAFIOSO CHRISTMAS
Mozzafiato, prequel to MAGARI

STAY CONNECTED
Find me here:

Let's stay connected. I'd love to hear what you thought of the book, what's on your TBR list, or simply how your day is going.

www.EleanorAldrick.com

Instagram
@EleanorAldrick

Goodreads
www.Goodreads.com/EleanorAldrick

Twitter
www.Twitter.com/EleanorAldrick

Facebook
www.Facebook.com/EleanorAldrick

Be sure to sign up for my newsletter where I share exclusive content. You won't want to miss out!

ACKNOWLEDGEMENTS
Thank You for everything!

Here we are again. At the end of a book and beginning of a new series. As I've come full circle on my author journey, I'd like to thank the one constant that's carried me through all of the tough times and has always encouraged me to keep going. My husband, my rock, and my friend. I love you to the moon and back. Thank you for all that you do.

I have to give a shout-out to two very special people who've helped make this book the very best it could be. There are no words that could express my gratitude for the encouragement, support, and feedback these two ladies have so graciously given me. Lauren and Suny, I'm so very blessed to call you my friends. Thank you for always keeping it real. I love you both to the moon and back!

I'd also like to thank my other real world, writing, and bookstagram besties. You keep me sane through the chaos, reminding me there's a light at the end of the tunnel. Taralyn, Nicole, Natalie, Ivette, Sara, Georgia, Marah, Alicia and Tracy, you ladies are rock stars and I appreciate each and every one of you.

Also, a massive thank you to everyone on my street team. Every share and every edit means so much to me. There's no way I would have the reach I do now without your help. You guys are Amazing!

Last but not least, I am beyond thankful for you. Thank you for taking a chance on my books. That alone has be overflowing with gratitude. Out of thousands and thousands of books, you chose to read my story. That right there is cause for celebration. So cheers to you, babe! Hopefully, this is just the start of our literary friendship.

XOXO, Eleanor Aldrick

Printed in Great Britain
by Amazon